The Ice War

Anders Blixt

DEDICATION

To my father.
He has taught me what is important in life.

CONTENTS

ACKNOWLEDGMENTS

Krister Lindholm, civilian peacekeeping expert in the Swedish army, played a major role in the making of this novella. During the Balkan wars in the 1990s, he recruited me for an administrative position at Swedint (the national HQ of our Blue Berets) and that job provided the insights I needed to write *The Ice War*. Sadly Krister passed away before its completion.

I would also like to thank Carolina Gomez Lagerlöf for an important revision suggestion. Four eyes see more than two.

PROLOGUE:

ALBA – A BRIEF INTRODUCTION

During the Classical Era many philosophers claimed that there must be a vast continent, called Terra Australis Incognita (Latin: "unknown southern land"), in the southern hemisphere to balance the landmasses of Europe, Asia, and Africa in the north. Medieval cartographers frequently inserted this hypothetical land in their maps.

The Dutch seafarers that explored the Southern Ocean during the 18th century discovered a new continent centred at the South Pole. Captain Pieter Jansen, who charted its coastlines in 1771-75, named it Terra Alba (Latin: "white land") for its icy wastes. During the 19th century, European geographers started using the shorter form Alba.

Alba has more than twice the surface area of Europe. Tall mountain ranges, vast ice plains, and dense forests of dark trees characterize its topography. It has extensive geological activity with smoking volcanoes in many locations and therefore earthquakes are common. Powerful eruptions have sometimes obscured the sky and chilled Alba's climate for years.

Alba's most distinctive geographical feature is Acheron, an enormous circular depression in the icy wastes. It is 12,000 feet deep and 1,500 miles in diameter and was probably created by a meteoritic impact many million years ago. At its bottom, air pressure and temperature are notably higher than at sea level. It therefore has a comparatively moderate climate, for instance with liquid water in the central salty Sea of Tears, and unique flora and fauna.

Alba's massive central ice sheet is surrounded by a tundra belt, with heaths, bogs and lakes. This zone receives about eight inches of precipitation a year, as little as many desert areas in other continents. But unlike the deserts, the tundra retains its water because there is little evaporation and a layer of permafrost keeps the water at the surface.

During summer melt water from the permafrost temporarily transforms vast areas into bogs. In those months the tundra displays a rich and colourful flora that supports a varied fauna. Most of these animals hibernate or migrate to the coasts during the cold seasons.

The ursines, also known as the bear-centaurs, are Alba's aboriginal intelligent population. They are stronger and bigger than humans and possess a similar intelligence. The ursines have reached the same level of technology as Europe in the 18th century, but their production is pre-industrial. They speak several languages and have developed writing indigenously, but illiteracy is widespread. The population density is low because of the harsh climate. Many ursines live as tribal nomads and herd zegut cattle across the tundra. The warmer Acheron is more densely populated and fragmented in many agricultural ursine realms. Some have been conquered by human powers, while others have voluntarily become protectorates in return for defence and trade arrangements, and a few remain independent.

The European powers have built a telegraph network that covers most of Alba's settled areas. The Habsburg Empire and Denmark have begun to build railroads. The ursines are not seafarers, but nowadays human steamers travel on the Sea of Tears. European technicians have also constructed juggernauts, huge steam- or diesel-powered vehicles that are used in flat wilderness regions and on the icy plains.

Two animals are particularly important to the tundra ursines: the native zegut and the Arctic husky. The nomads' way of life is governed by the migrations of their zegut herds between grazing areas. That animal's meat is considered to be a delicacy. Its hide is used for clothes and yurts, i.e., the nomads' hemispherical tents, and its bones for making tools. The huskies were introduced to the nomads by Danish and Russian explorers in the 19th century and gained widespread popularity as sled dogs.

Excerpt from Geography for Primary Schools *by Francis X. Nelson, Ph.D., Charleston, Carolina Colony, 1936. Reproduced with the publisher's permission.*

CHAPTER 1

The *Cassiopeia's* cargo ramp touched the ground with a clonk. I crossed it and stepped down on the cracked concrete of the landing pad. The cold wind smelled of burning coal and dusty roads. The sun stood halfway into the sky to the north-northwest: early afternoon local time. Carrion birds squabbled around a carcass at the nearest warehouse. Denmark's red and white flag fluttered over the cloudport's gate and beyond it I glimpsed Fredriksborg's cluster of dark buildings.

My destination was the desk for arriving cloudships in the customs office. The officer on duty spoke German with a thick Danish accent: "So you're coming from Magalhana? We haven't seen ships from there for a while. Why are you here, garçon?"

His slur did not surprise me and I responded with a well-rehearsed smile. "My name is Johnny Bornewald, Herr Zollwachtmeister," I said in cultured German. "We carry spare parts for the governor's office."

His eyes dodged my gaze. "The cargo manifest, garçon."

"At the bottom of this bundle, Herr Zollwachtmeister." I handed over a file with the ship's documents that the law required for arrivals at foreign cloudports. Some of the sheets were forgeries by our allies in the Dutch intelligence service, but I did not worry because before leaving the *Cassiopeia*, I had double-checked everything and found no flaws.

While the officer inspected the papers, I took a look at the surrounding office rooms and storage areas. They were mostly empty and unkempt with a few dirty machines that had not been used for a long time. Whatever cloudships arrived here must make do with on-board cargo-handling equipment. The cloudport had been built to handle ten or fifteen vessels at the same time, that was obvious, but after the outbreak of war in the northern hemisphere, incoming traffic must have fallen to next to nothing.

The document bundle hit the desk with a thud. I saw a blue clearance stamp at the top of the first page: FREDRIKSBORGS TOLDKONTOR, GODKENDT, 24 XI 1940.

"Tell your captain that everything is in order, garçon," said the officer.

I looked straight into his face when I picked up the papers. He turned away from me without the salute prescribed by his service regulations. I left the building without a "thank you" and took a few breaths of fresh air to rinse the bitter feelings out of my mind. In my current position I simply had to endure such treatment.

A grey Cloverland lorry with a partially disassembled biplane on the flatbed drove past me towards the main gate. The words SZENES MEKANIK A/S were stencilled in white on the cab door. A young woman in a blue overall handled the steering wheel; a proof that I had come halfway around the world, because females do not work as teamsters in Europe.

I have visited many shabby pioneer settlements in Africa and Magalhana, but Fredriksborg – a maze of three-story houses in black wood in the depths of Acheron – was more sombre, more crowded and colder. Each place has its fashion and its manners. This town was unfamiliar to me, so I had selected plain and practical dress: khaki trousers, a grey cotton shirt, a blue wool sweater, a blue winter jacket and a small backpack. A roll of Imperial thalers weighed heavily in a pocket, silver coins that are accepted in nooks and crannies all over the world.

Business practices resemble each other in general everywhere, but it is the small particulars of a place that matters. We were about to run into trouble in the Corli city-state in Magalhana, but fortunately we had realized in time how the system was skewed against foreign traders. We had departed before a court had had time to penalize us for some made-up misstep. It seemed that customs were nicer in Fredriksborg, because when I studied how people behaved in the bazaar, I got the impression that business transactions were handled in a polite and restrained manner. I was not harassed by vendors or beggars despite being an obvious stranger and the dark colour of my skin caused no adverse reactions, unlike in Europe where people frequently snub mischlings like me.

I strolled through the bazaar until I found my destination: Café Bleu, a hole-in-the-wall establishment in a long alley. The air inside was unpleasantly humid and some water dripped along a wall, probably from a leaky radiator. A blocky radio on a shelf was tuned to a station broadcasting romantic French music.

The proprietor, a short old Eskimo, nodded in my direction, stopped stacking plates and stepped forward behind the broad zinc counter.

"Good day," I said in German. "Black coffee, please. Do you have apple cake with vanilla sauce? I haven't had that…" – I inserted the prescribed brief pause to clear my throat – "…since the leaves fell in the English Garden." The current contact phrase according to the instructions that I had received before our departure from the Dutch East Indies.

The proprietor started to prepare a tray for me. "Autumn there … is spring here. But I always have apples in my larder." Correct response – contact established. He put a steaming cup and a plate with a cake slice on the tray. "One thaler, sir. Use the small table in the rear corner. You'll be left alone there."

I picked up my tray and headed in that direction, while the proprietor lifted a phone receiver and spoke in a low voice. With my back against the wall I let the eyes wander across the café. A gang of teens occupied the remaining three tables. Their mix of skin hues showed that Fredriksborg's population originated from all possessions of the Danish crown: Scandinavians, Eskimos, South Indians and Afro-Caribbeans. They were dressed in wide trousers and baggy colourful knitted sweaters according to some current fashion trend. One or two looked in my direction, but without suspicion. After all, my part-Indian looks blended well with the crowds. Outside people moved constantly back and forth, stopping every now and then to peek into the small shops along the alley.

I realized that it might take some time before my contact arrived, so I let my thoughts drift into the past: *A clattering propeller pushes a strong wind into my face. Far below me white waves beat at a wide sandy beach. My biplane heads north across the Pomeranian coast to the Baltic Sea. Destination: Gothenburg, Sweden. My first solo flight with the fresh pilot license in my leather jacket. An important rite of passage in my family, a proof of adulthood.* But this was only memories and I had not been to Sweden for years. Sometimes I longed to return, but I refused to live under the Russian yoke.

After eating half of the slice of cake, I pulled Ulrich Franke's heavy reference book *Alba: ein Handbuch* from the backpack. Soon I would be off on a long journey through icy wastes and the more I knew in advance, the better would my odds be. The European rebellion had not yet reached this continent, at least not as full-scale military operations, but it cast its shadow over the land.

Half an hour later a woman in a heavy coat entered the café, nodded at the proprietor and headed for my table. The Eskimo increased the volume of the music.

I got up to greet her.

The woman's dark eyes, striking in such a pale face, met mine without budging. "Hello. I'm Linda Connor." She spoke clear English, even though her R's burred in an unusual way, and shook my hand with a surprisingly firm grip for a slender person only five feet tall. I guessed she was about my age, thirty-something.

"Johnny Bornewald. Hello," I said in the same language. I had not expected to meet a woman, but she behaved as if her presence was natural. And shaking hands with an unknown dark-skinned man had not troubled here. *New continents, new customs*, I thought.

Linda moved dextrously when she shed the coat and revealed khaki trousers and a checked shirt underneath – a workman's dress. A long knife with a worn handle dangled from the belt. The combination of short black hair, male clothes and a slender physique gave her a boyish look.

The proprietor served her a cup of herbal tea while they exchanged pleasantries in Danish. I pretended not to understand. When he had left, Linda turned to me: "So, Mr. Bornewald, I've been instructed to assist you. What is your business?" She sounded like a civil servant handling an office matter, not like a wartime spy.

I answered in the same manner: "Industrial intelligence. My destination is Russia's Mine No 2 in the Montalban Mountains. I have orders to check its current production status. My cover is as an inspector for the mine's insurance company Société Générale d'Assurance carrying out an unscheduled safety check. You are to be my guide and we will go there overland by juggernaut."

"Why not charter an aeroplane?" she asked.

"I want to surprise them, to prevent them from hiding interesting matters. Aviators must file flight plans in advance and those might go astray before departure," I said. "Another matter, I need you as an interpreter, too, because I don't speak Russian."

"I grew up at a Russian estate with English-speaking parents so I'm bilingual. I also know German and Danish, because that's necessary in my trade," she said.

I nodded. "Good."

"When do you want to leave?" she said.

"Tomorrow if possible," I said.

"It's possible. But it'll be a long journey across the ice plateau. Do you have any experience of Arctic climate?"

She must have made a faulty assumption about my home country from my skin colour, I thought. "I grew up in northern Europe where winters are harsh. I know how to ski and skate, though I haven't done it for a few years."

"Good. See you at the railways station six o'clock tomorrow morning." A quick handshake over the table and then she left the café as quietly as she had arrived.

Captain Leclerc waited for me in his cabin. Its confined space reeked of tobacco smoke and not even a cold stream of air from a partially open porthole could disperse the acrid smell.

"Hello, Johnny." The captain spoke German out of politeness, because my Dutch was still halting. "A cigarillo?" He gestured toward small wooden box on his desk, partially hidden under mathematical tables, manuals and charts.

"No thanks, captain," I said.

"How did it work out?" he asked.

"Fine, captain. I'll be leaving tomorrow morning," I said.

"We must service the repeller and it may take weeks to get spare parts," Leclerc said. "So your absence won't be inexplicable."

I nodded. The *Cassiopeia's* landing had been so shaky that I had feared that she might crash.

He continued: "That incomplete overhaul in Karquim. Now we're paying for it."

I nodded again. On the other hand, we had had to flee that city prematurely because of the Empire's unexpected attack.

Leclerc rose from his chair, removed a panel above his bunk and fetched a thick envelope from a hidden compartment. When he moved around, his grey shock of hair almost touched the cabin's ceiling. He was not remarkably tall, but cloudships are cramped. "Here are your travel documents," he said.

I leafed through the papers: cover identities as an insurance inspector and as the *Cassiopeia's* trading agent. "Thanks, captain."

"Hals- und Beinbruch, Johnny."

I entered the cabin that I shared with signalman Willem Laan and started my coffee maker. My colleagues did not share my devotion to the art of brewing coffee, but viewed it as nostalgia. But I was ready to pay a lot for premium beans, because this was the only one of my old habits I still could indulge in.

Willem huddled in his bunk with a bundle of newspapers. He looked at me and ran the fingers across the scalp in an attempt to put his unruly black hair into place. "Hello. Did you see a barbershop somewhere in the port?"

"No, this place is just an empty shell. I only saw some customs and service people. You'll have to walk into town." I changed subject. "What's in the news? Anything I should worry about?"

Willem got out of the bunk and pointed at the map of Alba that I had attached to the bulkhead during the journey from the Dutch East Indies. White indicated ice plains, brown mountain ranges, light grey tundra, and dark grey taiga, whereas the solitary green roundel with a blue splotch in the middle outlined the huge Acheron crater with the Sea of Tears. Human settlements were identified by tiny flags.

He raised a pencil: "The news speaks of one a current political dispute. Here and here…" – the pencil touched two spots in a brown area – "…are the largest known coal deposits in Alba. Whoever controls them wields a lot of influence."

"Does it affect Fredriksborg?" I asked while pouring a cup of hot brew.

"Only indirectly," Willem said. "It is a dispute about land rights. When the European powers set up their settlements 30-40 years ago, those deposits had not been found. So the area was not carved up by treaty in the usual manner. And now the war has wrecked all old agreements. Fredriksborg imports coal, so its governor wants to maintain status quo for the time being."

"What's Russia's position?" I asked.

"To put her diplomatic gobbledygook in three words: 'leave us alone'," he said.

I sipped some coffee before responding: "Who quarrels with a bear?"

A flippant tone hid my rancour. As a boy I had seen king Peter's policemen use truncheons on women that demanded bread for their children in a street rally. I had cried without getting consolation, without getting understandable explanations for the cruelty. That night I had resolved to pursue a new course charted by my conscience: our society must change.

Soon I found out that my elder brother Abel already had made the same decision and together we entered the shady world of progressive dissenters. Conspiracies and malfeasance became routine when we helped refugees or acquired food for starving people.

After a few years we raised the stakes to risking our lives by smuggling a shipload of Jews to the Netherlands in foul weather. When disembarking, the parents thanked us for having saved their children from the ultras back home. That experience made me realize what it entailed to be an adult rather than a teenager, that is, to do what had to be done in the face of mortal danger. Life would never be the same again.

And then the republican rebellion erupted in the German countries and spread to Sweden. I was one of those who built cobble-stone barricades in the streets of Gothenburg and fought the police with improvised clubs and stolen shotguns. We dreamed of freedom during a brief summer, but in the autumn the tsar's Cossacks crossed the Baltic Sea "to restore order". Their knouts whirled in Sweden's shantytowns while the Okhrana hauled off real or imagined rebels to Siberia.

So I, too, fled to the Netherlands to carry on the struggle in other ways. Espionage became my weapon of choice, a shady business in which my education and broad experience paid off well.

CHAPTER 2

Fredriksborg's air is so polluted that its inhabitants only see the most luminous stars at night. But out on the ice sheet you see the full splendour of the night sky. My back rested against the railing that enclosed the observation deck of the juggernaut *Lady Margaret* while I admired the Milky Way's river of glittering dust. It was easy to identify our brilliant planetary neighbours Mars and Venus. Both Jupiter and Sirius were below the horizon at this hour, so the third strongest celestial sparkle ought to be Canopus. I had a hard time puzzling together the unfamiliar constellations of the southern hemisphere, but after a while I figured out which stars formed the Southern Cross and the adjacent Centaur.

Acrid smoke billowed from the *Lady Margaret's* funnel and covered a section of the sky where the sparks of smouldering coal fragments replaced the stars. Her steel-studded wheels rumbled incessantly and a cargo trailer clattered behind the stern. The din had kept me awake. After spending one hour with Franke's handbook in my bunk, I had decided to get some fresh air. On the way to the top deck I had walked through the canteen that occupied most of the upper deck of the passenger section. There I saw others who had hard time sleeping. A few people played cards and the bartender was doing brisk business. But I had not seen Linda. Most likely she was in her cabin, but I had no idea whether she was able to sleep – though as a mechanic she ought to be used to all this noise.

When Linda and I had met at Fredriksborg's railway station for the first stage of our journey, she had shown me a detailed travel plan. A steam train took us along a track winding up Acheron's shallow slope through a fertile farming area where ursines and humans worked side by side in the fields.

We travelled around the base of the dead volcano Hephaestus Mons. The air got thinner and colder with increasing altitude. Soon the train master activated the hot water radiators in the railcars and his men made sure that all windows were closed and sealed.

Hours later we had arrived at the Christianshus terminal, a building complex where passengers and cargo changed between the railroad and the juggernauts that travelled across the ice plains. Bunkers dotted the surrounding hills. Three tall military juggernauts had stood at the ice rim, angular armoured vehicles with many wheels and gun turrets. After all, this settlement was vital for Fredriksborg's communications with Alba outside Acheron, where the ice plains are as important as the seas in Europe.

The sun had just set with pink light still touching the volcano's snow-covered summit, when we disembarked the train to start the second stage of our journey, heading south via the mining towns of New Bristol and Novgorod.

A strong gust of wind suddenly chilled my face and shattered my reverie. *Time for another attempt to fall asleep*, I thought. *Maybe a nightcap will help.*

Weak light bulbs illuminated the canteen. I approached the bar, where the female bartender greeted me: "Guten Abend, mein Herr."

"Guten Abend," I said. "A vodka on the rocks, please."

While the bartender prepared the drink, I checked what other people were here. Four well-dressed men played cards at a big round table while having beer. They spoke German and from what I heard they knew each other well. I guessed that they were businessmen going to New Bristol.

A woman and a man conversed quietly at a bulkhead table with a pot of coffee between them. Both were in their thirties with similar robust clothes and crew-cut hairstyles. The tall man had a northern European hue, while the woman appeared to have both European and Oriental ancestry. Their composed and alert manner made me think of police and military officers. Their gestures indicated a level of intimacy, probably a married couple.

A forty-something European man in a white suit sat alone at another bulkhead with a drink in front of him. His face looked morose. *Someone else who cannot sleep*, I thought.

I selected an empty table at a porthole. The reflections of the light bulbs in the triple glass panes prevented me from seeing anything of the outside, provided that there had been anything to watch apart from ice and snow.

"Excuse me, sir." The man in the white suit approached me.

"Yes?" I said.

"You appear to be as bored as I am. May I join you for a chat?" He spoke educated English.

"Please do." Cloud travellers are used to tedious journey and one has to use whatever means available to keep oneself entertained.

"Peter Lee," he said and extended his hand.

"Johnny Bornewald."

"You're not from Alba, are you?" Lee asked.

"Why do think so?" I said.

"Your clothing." Peter Lee's breath smelled of alcohol and his face had the reddish hue of drunkenness. The drink he carried in his right hand was obviously not his first one this evening.

I reviewed Lee's mimics and speech and suspected that he, too, did not originate from Alba, but I kept quiet about my conclusion. "That's right."

I worried that he would start talking about what he thought was my native land, but instead he changed subject. "During daytime you can occasionally spot the leviathan hunters' ice-buggies. If we're lucky we might see one of those beasts. Have you already seen them?" When speaking he seemed less inebriated than I had feared.

"Well, only in photos." A leviathan looks like a mix of an enormous snail and a whale. Franke's handbook had explained that it subsists on pseudo-algae that grow as patches of green slime on the ice.

"You won't believe your eyes when you see one. Fifty-sixty yards long and ten yards tall. One of them would shatter *Lady Margaret* without noticing." He emptied his glass. "Do you know that people say that the leviathan hunters make a powerful aphrodisiac from a gland?"

A tall tale? Franke doesn't mention it, I thought. "No, I haven't heard that."

"The ursines hunt those beasts with muzzled-loaded cannons and it is easy to destroy that gland." Peter Lee started to ramble about the leviathans' role in the polar fauna.

I paid attention to his words, because I have learned the hard way that small facts every once in a while turn out to be vital. The more he spoke, the more I was convinced that he was from West Europe. He was a knowledgeable zoologist, but why this Alban specialisation? I had no idea, but I refrained from asking to avoid unwanted questions in return.

After half an hour I felt so tired that I decided to make another try at falling asleep. Peter Lee had ordered a new drink and seemed to be able to talk till dawn. When I left the canteen, he remained at the table, looking out into the darkness.

CHAPTER 3

"Calling Alpha One. This is Alpha Two. We're at Location Lambda. Over."
Short-wave radiotelephony has its drawbacks, for instance unpredictable
sound quality, but it is the most flexible method available if you want to
avoid public monopolies with telephone lines of questionable quality. My
radio was reliable, though quite a burden with its heavy lead batteries.

Leclerc grunted in response. It sounded as if I had woken him. "Alpha
One here. I read you, Alpha Two. Over."

"The journey is uneventful so far." I phrased my messages with care
because I had no idea who might be eavesdropping. "We plan to proceed to
Location Sigma presently. Over."

"Understood. Let me know when you have more precise plans. Alpha
One out."

New Bristol is situated in a flat area so the *Lady Margaret* left the ice sheet
and drove along a straight ice road to its juggernaut terminal. The place had
been colonized because of its plentiful high-quality iron ore.

Alba's towns look the same to an uninitiated visitor: shabby pioneer
settlements with houses of grey stone or black wood. But when you take a
closer look, you see that each possesses distinctive characteristics: the width
of the alleys, the colour schemes indoors, the inhabitants' dress code and
way of moving in public spaces, and so on. New Bristol seemed a bit
wealthier than Fredriksborg with less crowded alleys and more spacious
shops. It also had something that I had not seen in Fredriksborg: a metal
radio tower with a cluster of antennas reached for the sky next to the
terminal.

Linda had told me that leviathan hunters frequently visited New Bristol because of its convenient location at the ice sheet. When we had approached the coast just after dawn, I had waited at a porthole in *Lady Margaret's* canteen with the hope of seeing their ice-buggies, but unfortunately in vain.

Hotel Victoria consisted of three parallel corridors, joined by the reception area and other common facilities. Our two rooms were tiny, but the beds were comfortable and the staff accommodating and that is what weary travellers need.

In the evening I sat at my desk writing in my diary about our days in the *Lady Margaret*. I had listened to Peter Lee's ramblings at several occasions. When sober, he was less self-centred and had plenty to tell about Alba's flora and fauna. However, I avoided appearing too curious because I did not want to attract attention to me and Linda. The couple with the crew-cuts, Elsa and Leonard Schnittke, had alerted my suspicious mind. I had talked to them briefly once or twice and then they had claimed to be geologists heading for a mine. I did not believe them because of their military auras – their journey might instead be related to the simmering political crisis. Linda had preferred the solitude of her cabin, though we had shared several meals in the canteen. At those occasions, she had spoken much about Alba, but not a word about herself. On the other hand, I had not said much about my background. Rebels like anonymity.

A double knock on the door interrupted my writing and I responded: "Come in, please."

Linda entered and grabbed a chair. "I've spent some hours in the bazaar listening for local news," she said. "Someone said that a flier has reported an approaching squadron of ursine ice-buggies. They're expected to arrive just after dawn tomorrow. But nobody knew what clan they belong to, so I can't say whether these are people I'd want to talk to. Anyhow, let's watch that from the observation deck in the radio tower, shall we?"

"Good idea," I said.

The wide windows of the observation deck provided an all-around panorama. To east, the glittering ice sheet reached to the horizon. To the west a huge open-pit mine made me think of a pernicious lesion in the rolling snow-covered ground. Everywhere, at least so it seemed, smoke pillars rose from smelting furnaces and iron mills.

A group of third-graders in blue school coats swarmed around us under the watchful eyes of two teachers. I scanned the ice sheet through my binocular. The rising sun cast orange-yellow light cascades across the snow.

Linda's elbow touched me. "There!" She lowered her old-fashioned prism field-glass and pointed.

I reoriented my binocular while its whirring mechanisms adjusted for contrast and luminosity. Seven gaudy ice-buggies raced toward New Bristol's landing area. Each scrawny vehicle had a distinctive paintwork and fuselage layout with an enclosed crew cabin, long runners and spike-studded drive-wheels.

"The six striped ones belong to the Kirin clan, while the speckled one is from the Tairen," Linda said in German, probably to ensure that the kids would not understand. "An unexpected alliance."

"How come?" I said in the same language.

"The Kirin are dark-furred and usually do not travel with pale-furs like the Tairen. The Kirin territory is nearby, whereas the Tairen live further south and rarely turn up here," she said.

"Are they enemies?" I asked.

"No, but the Tairen craft must have come here for some particular reason," she said.

I scanned the land closer to the observation tower. A narrow promontory extended about four hundred yards into the ice just north of the place where *Lady Margaret* had rolled off the ice sheet. Its surface was uneven with occasional black bushes growing out of the snow. I noticed a movement near its tip and adjusted the magnification of the binocular. Its gyros started whirring to keep it steady during zooming. A human in white wilderness clothing, facing away from me, crouched near the ice beach in a location that could not be observed from the west. However, the observation deck was so high above the ground that neither cliffs nor shrubberies obstructed my line of sight.

That person must have walked from New Bristol so I started searching for tracks in the snow. I found none, but I noticed two other humans in white advancing out on the promontory. Currently they were about three hundred yards from the crouching individual but they should not be able to see him from their current position.

I zoomed out. The six Kirin ice-buggies drove past the promontory and followed its southern edge toward the landing, whereas the Tairen vessel rushed for the tip. The roof of its crew cabin flipped open, revealing two drivers and two riflemen to my enhanced gaze. It veered twenty yards from land and skidded to a halt with ice dust spraying from the runners. The waiting human dashed toward it, but stumbled after a few steps and fell head over heels on the ice. I quickly checked the other humans. They crouched with rifles in firing positions among ice boulders on the north side of the promontory, about two hundred yards from the Tairen ice-buggy.

One rifleman in that vehicle opened fire and a cloud of black-powder smoke billowed from his repeater. The other one got down on the ice and lifted the fallen human aboard. Meanwhile the six Kirin ice-buggies swerved left in tight formation and hit the south edge of the promontory. The two snipers must have heard them, because they started to retreat using whatever cover they could find.

As soon as the wounded human was inside the Tairen buggy, it bolted for the open ice sheet with ice fragments flying from its drive wheels. Its two riflemen held their fire, probably because they risked hitting the Kirin ursines who had jumped out of their vehicles and now stormed the promontory in a military manner.

The two snipers withdrew skilfully among rocks, ice boulders and bushes. I was sure that I was watching Mr and Mrs Schnittke in action. They had the advantage of firing smokeless ammunition, while their adversaries used black-powder rounds. They soon knocked out one ursine and while the others hit the ground, they disengaged using smoke grenades to obscure their movements.

They are rushed, otherwise they would not have open fire so close to a town, I thought. *Why?*

When the couple got off the promontory, they headed north and I lost them behind a cluster of black shrubberies. After two minutes the ursines trotted back to their ice-buggies, carrying their wounded comrade, and the squadron departed at high speed. The gunshots had not been audible in the observation chamber and the event had been so far away that nobody without binoculars would have been able to figure out what really had happened. The school children had not understood anything, but the teachers talked to one another about what they thought they had seen.

Linda, putting the field-glass in her backpack, said: "Let's leave now, before the police get into action."

I nodded and followed her to the tower's elevator.

CHAPTER 4

"According to news bulletins from Europe, republican and imperial forces are engaged in a major battle in northern Hungary. The Imperial Ministry of War in Vienna has announced that this is a part of an offensive to secure vital railway lines. The reports of the two adversaries are contradictory: both claim that the enemy is facing an imminent defeat.

"Edvard Beneš, president of Bohemia, said in a speech broadcast yesterday to the Central European republics that he expects no quick end to the battle for liberty, but that the superior morale and technology of the republican alliance will ensure that its success. He also called for more volunteers to enlist, saying: 'So far we have been spared the disgrace of mandatory conscription.'

"As for the shooting incident this morning near the ice landing, the police have so far failed to identify who were involved, apart from the presence of unknown Kirin clansmen. The police see no connections to local criminal activities.

"A week ago Juliusburg's leader Eric Terboven said in a speech commemorating the seventh anniversary of the establishment of that settlement that his corporation had no territorial claims vis-à-vis Novgorod, but that the current dispute concerning the exploitation of coal deposits in the Montalban range must be settled in a manner that fully respects the rights of Juliusburg.

"The transport bureau has purchased two new cargo juggernauts for…"

I switched off the radio. A republican defeat in Hungary would have serious consequences for the rebellion's heartlands in Bohemia, Saxony and Hessen. Beneš was a sensible leader and I interpreted his message as a warning to the citizens of the republics: matters were about to get worse.

17

"What do you think of that Terboven?" I said.

"A despotic director in the Rhodes Conglomerate. I know that his henchmen have slaughtered ursines that refused to 'resettle' at the corporate latifundios. But so far, he hasn't attacked other human settlements," said Linda.

I sensed that the great rebellion was about to set Alba on fire. "Time to get back on the ice, isn't it?"

Linda nodded.

Linda and I stood at the wide stern window in the salon of the juggernaut *Ekaterina* and watched New Bristol's billowing smoke plumes at the horizon. After the news broadcast Linda had bought tickets for Novgorod with departure the same day and the police had not approached us before we left. Now I looked forward to a few eventless days on the ice sheet.

Linda gripped the railing with the face close to the glass, so I did not see her face, but her shoulders were tense.

"When was your last visit to Novgorod?" I asked.

"A while ago," she said.

"What's the place like?" I said.

"So and so," she said.

I got the hint and switched subject: "Alba is white and lifeless. My home is verdant green and brown." I did not know whether she paid attention to me, but I continued regardless. "Here and there you see grey outcrops of bedrock. In other places tarns and lakes that mirror the sun and the clouds."

"Do you sometimes feel like going back?" she mumbled without looking at me. That was the first time she inquired about my background.

"Certainly. But I don't want to live in an occupied ruin. Instead I have come to live in a cloudship," I said.

"Is that better?" she said.

"I think so." My eyes wandered over the ice, where *Ekaterina's* steel-studded wheels were carving an interminable scar. The black cargo trailer was a wheeled rectangular box on the white. Far away, I glimpsed the top of New Bristol's communication tower. But that was all.

The day before the *Ekaterina's* arrival in Novgorod, she was intercepted by a military juggernaut.

Linda and I were having lunch in the stern salon. During the last few days our conversation had become more relaxed. She spoke occasionally of past experiences, such working in a juggernaut's engine room or watching how ursines hunted leviathans. The rough life of a plebeian woman, always

18

close to poverty; well, I had fallen from the peaks of society to that level. But I still hoped to be able to return to a less wearisome existence after the war, whereas that was beyond her imagination.

When I looked out at the ice through the stern window I saw a column of black smoke port abaft. "We're getting company," I said in English.

Linda looked in the same direction. "Check her flag, please."

I walked up to the railing for a better view. The pursuer, a tall white vessel with angular gun turrets, advanced noticeably faster than the *Ekaterina*. A few other passengers came up beside me while conversing in Russian.

My binocular was in my cabin, so I had to strain my naked eyes against the glitter from the ice. "The top mast displays a four-coloured flag: orange, white, blue, and green," I said.

"The Orange State. That juggernaut is from Juliusburg," said Linda.

A message lamp blinked at the pursuer's bridge. I understood nothing of the dash-dot code – the message was probably in Russian. A few seconds later, a voice addressed the passengers from the salon's loudspeaker, first in Russian and then in poor English: "This is executive officer Churkin. We are hailed by military juggernaut *Panther* from Juliusburg. Her captain asks for permission to search our vessel for wanted criminals. Captain Gorky has decided to comply. We will halt here for about twenty minutes. On behalf of captain, I apologize for any inconvenience."

During this address the *Ekaterina* braked to a standstill. The *Panther* stopped on our port side with two turrets pointing in our direction. I glimpsed two men on her bridge watching our vessel through binoculars. A steel hatch opened close to the ice and six men in white anoraks and trousers got out. Five carried white-painted carbines while the sixth had a revolver holstered at the belt – probably an officer. They walked briskly to *Ekaterina*, their grey boots making heavy imprints in the shallow snowdrifts on the ice.

Are they looking for us? I thought. *Is my cover shattered?* I turned to Linda. "What do you think they're interested in?"

"Probably weapons heading for Novgorod. Anyhow, this is a breach of the sea and ice law, but what can the captain do?" Linda looked troubled, despite her formal way of speaking.

I returned to the table. Metallic noise from below indicated that one of *Ekaterina's* main hatches opened for the inspection patrol. Ten minutes passed; the waiter roamed the salon, pretending that everything was normal while he refilled glasses and teacups. Every once in a while I looked at the Panther, but nothing happened there.

The double door toward the cabin section opened and a soldier in white entered, his Steyr carbine pointing at the deck. A Juliusburg officer with a major's oak leaf on the collar followed right behind, a grim-looking man whose eyes seemingly never blinked. Another soldier and one of the *Ekaterina's* junior officers were the last to enter.

The major addressed the passengers in German with an odd, almost Dutch accent: "Good day. Ladies and gentlemen, I am major Hout of Juliusburg's army. We are looking for wanted criminals." He leafed through a small black notebook while scrutinizing us civilians. Everyone was silent.

I shivered as I worried: *He must be comparing us to photos. Will he take a close look at me?*

After a minute or two the major closed the notebook. "I believe everything is in order. I regret any inconveniences. Adieu."

I exhaled. *Next time we won't escape so easily.*

I looked out through the stern windows. Two soldiers and two of the *Ekaterina's* crewmen inspected the contents of the cargo trailer. *It is not heated, so they are not looking for humans or ursines* I thought.

Officer Churkin's estimate turned out to be fairly correct. After twenty-five minutes, the *Ekaterina* resumed her journey. The *Panther* departed a few minutes later on a course away from us. I watched her smoke plume till it disappeared in the distance.

CHAPTER 5

I opened my eyes. My body felt sweaty and chilly at the same time. The nap had been shallow, troubled by hectic dreams whose images vanished from my memory seconds after waking up. A diesel engine thumped underneath me and my seat trembled – the field omnibus was still on the way to our destination. It travelled on a miserable excuse for a road, but at least its suspension had been designed to cope with that. The cabin radiators were connected to the cooling system of the engine and leaked a little, which made the air unpleasantly humid.

According to my wristwatch, it would be at least half an hour till our arrival at Mine No 2 in the Montalban range. Linda sat next to me at a window and looked out at the snow-covered hills. The pane fogged over quickly so she had to rub her sleeve against it every now and then.

Two grey-clad policemen with well-nourished faces sat at the front of the passenger cabin. The other travellers, mostly bearded miners in worn brown overalls, dozed or chatted while passing around vodka bottles and pretending that the officers were invisible.

The morning news had reported that the talks between the delegations of Juliusburg and Novgorod had been adjourned. The weather forecast predicted Force 2 winds and temperatures around $-30°C$.

"Did you sleep well?" Linda asked me in English.

"No, too much rattling," I said and leaned in front of her to get a glimpse of the world outside. This part of the Montalban was low and undulating. A copse of black scrawny coniferous trees grew in the snow next to the road. I remembered that Franke's handbook had described this species as a single organism whose multiple trunks were connected by an underground root system. Its metabolism was based on alcohols, so it would not perish from strong cold. Its black surfaces absorbed light efficiently. The roots were hard as copper and could burrow slowly through the permafrost.

"Andrei Yazov, Chief Mine Administrator," a sign proclaimed in Russian and German on the desk. The office was spare and its bookshelves displayed volumes in many languages. Mr Yazov spoke excellent German and wore a bespoke suit with a conservative cut. I shook his hand and sat down in a plush visitor's chair. A servant put two cups of tea on the small table between us.

"Herr Bornewald, I hope that engineer Churbanov's tour of our facilities was satisfactory." Yazov's face and eyes displayed nothing beyond professionalism. "Perhaps some of my men did not understand fully what a risk inspector is supposed to check."

I nodded and sipped some tea before answering. "I am satisfied with how accommodating everyone has been and your facilities are impressive." The working conditions underground were harsh but the sophisticated heating systems ensured that the air in the pits maintained endurable temperatures.

"Here are a few examples of our production." Yazov opened a small flat box and put a row of tiny metal bars on the table. They were stamped with chemical designation, weight and purity: platinum, palladium, osmium, and iridium – metals of great importance for advanced military technology.

I started to respond, but a sudden clatter of gunshots interrupted me. Instinctively I dived for the floor. When I had gathered my wits half a second later, I saw that a perplexed Yazov remained in the chair. He said something in Russian.

"I don't speak Russian!" I said in German.

Yazov started getting on his feet when more firearms banged nearby, both rifles and machine guns. Two cannon blasts rattled the window panes. The room's main door swung open.

Hell, I thought. *Here they come.*

But it was Linda crawling in. "Battle-wagons from Juliusburg are inside the compound," she said in English.

By now, Yazov too had hit the floor. He shouted a question at Linda and she answered. I only understood the words *Juliusburgskaya armiya* so I shouted: "Speak a language I know!"

"I just caught a glimpse of the vehicles through the window in the anteroom," said Linda in German.

"A surprise attack. I've got not warning," Yazov said in the same language. He breathed heavily and his face was red. "War has begun."

"Any garrison around here?" I said.

"No, and we cannot defend ourselves, because my men are in the pits." Yazov's voice faltered. It seemed that he had a hard time making phrases in German. "They are trapped. The enemies can kill them by shutting down the heating."

Running boots thudded in a nearby corridor. The servant entered through a side door. He looked frightened and Yazov addressed him in rapid Russian. The man nodded, picked up a white napkin and left through the main office door.

"I told him to get hold of an enemy officer and take him here so that I can put an end to the fighting," said Yazov. He got up and brushed some dust from his suit.

Linda and I remained on the floor, because staying low is always wise in a firefight.

The servant returned and started a whispering conversation with Yazov at the main door. I decided to use the chaos to my advantage, got on my feet and stole four of Yazov's metal bars. After all, they possessed what spies call "significant intelligence value".

Many footsteps in the anteroom – four soldiers in dirty white anoraks entered the office, three with rifles, and the fourth with a revolver. Their boots left wet prints on the teak floor. I recognized the uniforms from the encounter with Panther.

Yazov waited for them standing behind his desk with a straight back, but his cheeks were still red and sweaty.

"I'm captain Lawrence Dundee," said the man with the revolver to Yazov in English, "deputy commander of the battalion that has captured your mine." The dialect indicated that he was from Virginia.

A mercenary, I thought.

Dundee paid no attention to Linda and me, but one of his men turned to us and raised his rifle.

"We're unarmed," said Linda in English and started shivering and crying. Since I knew what kind of woman she was, I realized that she was acting. However, the soldier did not lower his rifle.

"My name is Andrei Yazov and I am in charge here." Yazov's voice was calmer now, though his English sounded uncertain.

"Juliusburg has occupied this mine and you are personally responsible for your men's behaviour. Resisters and saboteurs will be shot. Now, give me all keys to your gun lockers," ordered Dundee.

Yazov nodded and opened a drawer in the desk. He handed over a set of keys. "Do you know where they are located?"

"Yes." Dundee put away the keys in a pocket. "I'll use the anteroom as a command post. From now on, you'll report to me."

"How many of my men are dead or wounded?" asked Yazov.

"I don't know, but the takeover was painless." Dundee sounded indifferent. "My men mostly fired warning shots."

Yazov looked relieved.

"Now, Mr Yazov, I want you to address your men in the pits via your loudspeaker system. They must come up and be accounted for. If they make trouble, we'll shut off the heating. I'll put some Russian-speaking soldiers at your side to make sure you're not cheating." Dundee turned toward me. "Ty panemáyeš po angliski?" His Russian had a strong accent.

I guessed the meaning of his question from its last word – angliski ought to mean English – and nodded.

"Remove that hysterical woman and return to you tasks, garçon."

Without a word I lifted Linda, who put her arms around my neck. I carried her through the office building, which now was crowded with soldiers. They were busy eating and drinking tea or coffee. Apart from rude comments in Afrikaans or English, they let us be.

I continued through the covered passage to the hostel building, where Linda and I had been assigned one small guest room each. Through a window I saw the open area between the main buildings. A white battle-wagon with the Orange banner flying from the radio aerial stood there with the angular gun turret swivelling back and forth. Its studded wheels had ripped long tracks in the frozen ground. A corpse lay in a blood-stained snow heap, one of the local security guards judging from the uniform. Some soldiers in dirty white uniforms and arctic helmets with face covers locked in combat position were checking the civilian vehicles parked at the far end of the open area.

Linda had stopped crying, but she pressed her face against my ribs. I entered the hostel through its cold-weather lock. Some soldiers occupied the reception and one of them looked at me with contempt in his face.

Before he opened his mouth, I addressed him in English with a phony Russian accent: "My colleague has been frightened out of her wits. I will try to make her calm down."

"Go ahead, garçon, but don't do anything stupid. We shoot trouble-makers on the spot."

I carried Linda upstairs to her room on the second story. She slid out of my arms, opened the door and we sneaked in. The room had not been touched. The air had a stale smell – the ventilation system was probably out of order.

"Good acting," I said.

She smiled. "Just exploiting men's prejudices."

Pain shot through my belly – too much strain. *How do we get out of this mess?* I considered using the radio to speak to *Cassiopeia*, but discarded the idea, because alerting eavesdropping Juliusburgian radio operators would be dangerous. If the attackers caught us, we would be shot as spies.

I pushed aside our luggage, which had been deposited here by the hostel staff at our arrival, and got into the sole easy chair. "Right now, nobody will bother with us. It'll take hours before they've counted and interned all the miners. But as soon as Dundee's men realize we're not a part of the regular crew, we'll be interrogated. Maybe they'll make a prisoner exchange?"

"My people in Fredriksborg won't be able to help us," said Linda.

"My captain might be able to pay for our release. But he's far away and the *Cassiopeia* is grounded for repairs." We are stranded in the middle of a war. "How do we escape?" Despair flooded through my mind. "You're the one to know."

Linda sighed and cursed in Russian: "Kčortu!"

CHAPTER 6

A moon-lit lifeless snowscape outside the windows – the occupiers spent the night indoors, apart from a few patrols. After all, what sane miner would attempt to flee into the freezing wilderness? Mars glittered near the western horizon. I felt extra alert thanks to a pink Maxidin pill from my medicine kit.

I gripped the red emergency handle; in Alba's ice zone you open outside windows only in extreme circumstances. One jerk and the window swung open. A gust of wind, straight out of Dante's frozen hell, swept into the room, but Linda and I were protected by polar suits. I squeezed through the narrow opening and slid down to the ground six feet below.

The snow squeaked under the soles. I scanned the surroundings – all was calm. The snow on this side of the building was untouched by human boots. I glanced at the watch to check local time and temperature: an hour after midnight and about $-25°C$.

I extended a hand toward the window. Linda handed over two backpacks that I put on the ground. Then I positioned myself with the back against the wall. Linda slid out over the window sill and put her feet on my shoulders. She leaned into the room and grabbed the exterior emergency handle, pulled the window into place and locked it – no cold draught would reveal our escape.

After shouldering our backpacks, we proceeded to the left along the wall toward a garage. At the corner of the hostel, we faced a gap of thirty yards with no cover. A squad of patrolling soldiers vanished around a tall building sixty yards to the left. Indistinct sounds indicated that people were busy at the miners' barracks, but intervening buildings obstructed the line of sight

26

in that direction. No military vehicles around – the nearest one ought to be on the other side of the hostel.

My hand signalled "all clear" to Linda and we crossed the open area quickly, the snow squeaking every time a boot touched the ground. Running would be an unwise idea, because that would instantly alert anyone glimpsing us, but it was hard to keep a restrained pace on the exposed ground.

Quickly we reached the stone wall of the garage and slunk to the side that faced away from the compound. Its only door had a window above the doorframe. I saw a weak light behind the pane, but whether that indicated the presence of people – well, we would have to gamble now.

We approached the door. "Get on top of me and check," I whispered to Linda.

She removed the backpack, climbed onto my shoulders and replied in a barely audible whisper: "There is one bulb burning, but I see no people. There are a few vehicles." She slid to the ground and I leaned towards her face mask to hear her assessment: "Three snowcats and two snowmobiles. We should steal the snowmobiles because they are the fastest ice vehicles around here."

"Great. We have to get moving before someone spots our footprints in the snow," I said.

"Do you know how to drive a snowmobile?" Linda asked.

"Yes, but I haven't done it for a few years," I said. Actually for more than ten, but I hoped it would be like bicycling, that is, a skill that you never lose once you have acquired it. I pulled the auto-picklock out of my backpack. It slipped into the lock and I coaxed it gently. It clicked for a few seconds and fell silent. I turned it and opened the door.

Linda and I entered the building and unstrapped our arctic face masks. The air smelled of grease, coal and detergents. The garage was well maintained and fairly warm, one or two degrees above freezing. Tool racks filled one wall and heavy appliances occupied a corner, everything labelled Russian. The three red snowcats and the two yellow snowmobiles faced the wide main door, apparently ready to depart.

"How many clever things are in your backpack?" asked Linda.

"More than anyone would imagine." I tried to use a light-hearted tone. "I've learned a few things about survival since the rebellion began." But not enough about polar survival; dodging death right now required Linda's skills.

Linda mumbled something inaudible while walking over to check the snowmobiles. Their driver compartments were fully enclosed and Linda explained that the interior was heated by air circulating around the engines.

I started looking for petrol. "How do you write 'fuel' in Russian?"

Linda pointed at four red barrels beyond the snowmobiles. "That's what you're looking for. Anyhow, the fuel tanks of the snowmobiles are topped. About ten gallons each. Will take us a thousand miles or so."

"We should drive out that way," I said and pointed at the door through which we had entered. "The safest route into the hills."

Linda nodded and we started dragging the snowmobiles into starting positions.

The chuffing engines spread foul-smelling fumes inside the garage. Linda signalled "go ahead". I opened the door, backed three steps, and got seated in the snowmobile's saddle. The vehicles lumbered ahead, screeching loudly, across the threshold. As soon as my snowmobile hit the snow, I turned the throttle to max and rushed forward with Linda on my tail.

The rolling terrain ahead was almost devoid of vegetation. My snowmobile trembled when I pushed it to the limit. Our first goal was to get behind the nearest ridge fifty yards away. I glimpsed that Linda was moving up next to me to the right. *If a battle-wagon spots us...* I quickly interrupted that train of thoughts to focus on my driving.

Side by side we crossed the ridge and the low buildings in the compound disappeared out of sight. However, someone switched on a searchlight mounted on a pole tall enough to look over the ridge. The bright beam wandered across the terrain behind us. Suddenly two soldiers appeared in the moonlit landscape about thirty yards in front of us. The right one raised his hand in a "stop" gesture, while the other moved his rifle into firing position. I cajoled some extra power from the engine while aiming the snowmobile at the rifleman. He fired a snapshot with no apparent effect and tried to dodge, but I twisted the handlebar and rammed him. The snowmobile shuddered and tossed his body to the side.

The next ridge lay thirty yards ahead. I glanced to the right: Linda drove line abreast with me and made a "thumbs up". The rear-view mirror revealed nothing about the soldiers' fate. Somewhere a heavy machine gun rattled, but I saw no muzzle flashes. *A frightened soldier firing at shadows,* I thought.

We darted across the second ridge. The immediate danger should now be over, but our wide tracks in the snow would aid every pursuer. Many hours had to pass before we would dare take a break, but right now neither of us would tire for a long time. As for the inevitable Maxidin hangover, that would be a later worry.

We stopped at dawn for breakfast. After the first dash away from the mine, we had cut our speed to eleven knots to reduce the risk for accidents. Linda has assumed the lead because she had more ice-driving experience. We stayed away from the main road to Novgorod. Instead we let the stars guide us through the Montalban wilderness: white snow, never-ending hills and lifeless desolation under a glittering black sky. Man would always be an alien here.

I idled the engine to keep the passenger compartment warm, strapped the face mask in place and got out. The temperature remained at $-25°C$. A southerly breeze pushed scattered clouds across the sky. The sun climbed slowly up from the eastern horizon. A silent landscape – nothing to hear but our engines and the wind. I eased my stiff joints by stretching and bending. Linda got out, too, and began a t'ai chi ch'uan exercise, gliding like a fairy on the snow despite the bulky polar suit.

"I think we've covered about sixty miles," I said.

Linda answered without interrupting her moves: "I've managed to keep a fairly straight course. All the valleys in this area seem to run toward the ice sheet."

I pulled my backpack out of the small bonnet. "I'll fix some breakfast." My camping stove quickly transformed a mix of freeze-dried food and snow to an almost proper meal.

Two people could barely eat together inside the snowmobile compartment, provided that one of them pressed the back against the handlebar – I acted like a gentleman and slid into that position. The aroma of mushroom soup filled the air.

"Do you think he died?" Linda lowered her cup and look at the snowscape.

"No idea. I drove as fast as I could when I rammed him. But I saw no more," I said. *What do say you after killing someone?* I found no answer to that question, never had, never will. Instead I said: "Let me fill your cup."

After the breakfast, I burned all papers connecting me to Société Générale d'Assurance. When fleeing in a war zone, it is wise to have only one cover identity. And working for the *Cassiopeia* was the better option, because Leclerc would be able to verify that claim straight away.

"Johnny, I can't drive anymore." Linda's voice sounded as weary as her statement.

I put supper on her plate. "I understand. You're having a Maxidin hangover. I don't feel any better myself." My eyes could not focus properly and an ache pulsated inside the skull.

"We've covered ninety or more miles and ought to be close to the ice sheet," Linda said.

"You know what to do to survive a night out here." The food in my mouth garbled my voice. Maxidin stimulates one's hunger badly and I could not stop munching.

"We'll make a small igloo before the sun sets," Linda said.

After toiling for an hour with the igloo, I was close to collapse. I unfolded the sleeping pads on the packed snow and put the sleeping bags in place. The camping stove had raised the inside temperature to an endurable level. We would most likely sleep well.

Linda crawled into her sleeping bag. Her face was pale and the hands trembled.

"Where are we going tomorrow?" I asked.

"We must find some nomads. We can't go on like this on our own. We have to go north now. Juliusburg's military must be patrolling the ice sheet to blockade Novgorod." Linda's voice was weak.

"Sure, but how?" I said.

In that moment she fell asleep. For the first time I saw her face at peace. Now I knew what she had looked like before the rebellion began.

I closed the opening of my sleeping bag, leaving only my nose and eyes exposed to the chill air. Just before my mind fell asleep, I recalled the soldier that I had rammed. That mental picture would remain with me for the rest of my life.

CHAPTER 7

Breakfast in bright sunlight after fourteen hours' solid sleep: despite our miserable situation, I felt buoyant. After reviewing the poor maps we possessed, Linda and I agreed that the ice sheet ought to be no more than eight miles away.

Our route would take us down along a shallow valley covered by an immobile river of ice with mid-sized hills and ridges flanking it on both sides. My binocular pinpointed occasional black bushes on those hilltops. A glitter beyond the farthest hills – sunlight reflected from the ice sheet – signalled where the next stage of our journey would begin.

Linda and I packed the equipment and checked the vehicles. We worked in silence and I noticed the team spirit we had developed: not once did we interfere with each other's movements.

Linda brushed the snow from her polar suit and made a "thumbs up" gesture. The engines started with no problems and she drove up in front of me. The sun stood low to our right and the snowmobiles cast long shadows on the shining snow. *Less than an hour to the ice sheet*, I thought.

The hidden machine gun rattled for less than a second. Bullets drew an uneven line in the snow in front of us. Ice fragments sprayed for a moment from the impacts before the wind dispersed the glittering dust. Both Linda and I stopped our snowmobiles abruptly.

Hell! My belly turned into a cold knot. *Where is it?!* I put the engine on idle, strapped the face mask in place and got out, keeping my hands very visible to show that I was unarmed. The snow squeaked with each step as I turned to scan the area around us.

31

The valley along which we had been driving had made a turn to the left just before the salvo. We had been driving in the open, ignoring the miniscule risk of encountering enemies in the middle of nowhere. The valley ran straight ahead after the curve and it was more than two hundred yards wide. I scanned the ice blocks and uneven spots on the hillsides with my binocular, but the gunners had made a good job: I did not find their strongpoint.

I noticed a movement to my left and zoomed in that direction. Two soldiers with rifles on their backs skied down the slope toward us. On the ridge above them, more than one hundred yards away, I glimpsed a camouflaged military post. That must be the location from which we had been observed when approaching this section of the valley. We must have been spotted several minutes before that well-hidden machine-gun opened fire.

The soldiers skidded to a halt about ten yards from me. I did not recognize their polar uniforms or their cold-weather visor helmets, but when one of them addressed me in Russian, bile rose in my throat. I shook my head to show that I did not understand the words.

The Russian switched to bad German: "We from Novgorod. Who you?"

I answered in the same language: "We are refugees from the war."

The soldiers made a fumbling attempt to continue the discussion, but gave in and waved at the post on the summit. A soldier got out and headed downslope on skis. Meanwhile the other soldiers approached the snowmobiles and took a close look at them. Linda gazed back at him from her seat.

The third Russian stopped near me and opened his visor. "Good day. I am sergeant-major Firsov of the Russian army," he said in decent German. The rifle remained on his back.

I responded: "Good day. I am Johnny Bornewald and my travelling companion is Linda Connor. We were on a trading trip to Novgorod and visited Mine No 2 in the Montalban range when Juliusburg attacked. We managed to escape last night."

"From where do you originally come?" Firsov said in a stern voice.

"Miss Connor is from Fredriksborg. I am from the Netherlands," I said.

"How were you able to escape?" said Firsov.

"The occupiers had to sort out several hundred miners. They had no time to pay attention to us and we used that opportunity. And we had some luck," I said.

"I understand," said Firsov and made an impatient gesture at Linda. She strapped her face mask in place and got out of the snowmobile.

Meanwhile the second soldier started rummaging through my backpack, which he had found in the bonnet. I hoped that he would not realize what it contained, because I did not want to explain the purposes of some of my possessions.

When Linda stood at my side, Firsov addressed her in German. She responded in Russian and a brief discussion ensued. Firsov concluded it with a sharp sentence and turned to me. "I think you two can be of use," he said in German. "You will be escorted to our juggernaut. My men will ride with you in the snowmobiles." He looked down the valley and waved at some hidden observer. "So, get moving!"

The Russian military juggernaut *Sovremennyy* was a white behemoth on huge steel wheels, parked next to a bluff at the edge of the ice sheet. The tsar's naval flag fluttered over the bridge: a white cloth with a blue St Andrew's cross. Soldiers clung to its sides, repairing battle damage. The stern-most of the four gun turrets appeared to have been wrecked by a direct hit. No smoke rose from the funnels, so the engines must be shut down.

The bluff veered inland behind the juggernaut's stern, making room for a narrow flat beach. Half a dozen white tents had been erected in a strict formation on the edge of the beach together with a chuffing generator. Fifty yards inland, I saw a cairn of newly-cut ice blocks next to a tall orthodox cross of iron.

We parked the snowmobiles next to a sentry at the tents. One of our escorts reported something to him and then addressed Linda with an instruction in Russian. She translated it for me: "We will now meet major Akhmatov."

The major's lair inside a tent consisted of a rickety foldable desk with neatly stacked papers next to a vacuum flask and a cup of steaming tea. A kerosene stove kept the temperature above freezing, so he and his colleagues were able to work without face protection.

"Welcome," said Akhmatov in crisp English and shook hands. The grip was firm, his back was tall and straight and the eyes full of confidence. The deep furrows carved into his face showed that he worked for many years in harsh climate. He asked me to fetch two foldable chairs stacked at the rear of the tent.

"We are unfortunately in trouble," he said. "We encountered an enemy yesterday. Soon we'll be on the move again. So I have to rush our meeting and cannot show customary hospitality. But would you like some tea?" He filled two cups from the flask. It was a tasty brew, probably Ceylonese, though a bit too sweet for my liking. For a minute we heard only the humming of the heater's fan.

"Well, Mr Bornewald and Miss Connor, what are you doing in the middle of the wilderness?" asked Akhmatov.

I told him our story without lying and without giving away anything sensitive. He made notes without commenting. When I had finished, he put his notebook on the table and looked at me. "Mr Bornewald, this is not a credible."

"I've been in trouble before. I know that it's better to flee when bullets start flying." He was a veteran in his field so I decided to play the game his way.

"I've heard such claims before," he said.

I did not budge. "If you think I'm lying to you, what do you think the truth would be?"

"Well that's a good question. Terboven recruited many mercenaries before the start of the hostilities," he said.

"I realize that you don't want get in touch with the *Cassiopeia* by radio." Akhmatov nodded.

"My business plan is in my backpack," I said.

"Get it," he said.

While I headed outdoors, Akhmatov started talking to Linda in Russian. During my walk to the snowmobiles, I saw that soldiers were disassembling the tents. When I opened my backpack to get my business diary, I checked the contents – nothing missing.

Back in the tent, I handed over the diary to the major. He read it for several minutes, closed it, and said: "Well, I believe you. According to the laws and customs of war I hereby declare you to interned civilians of non-combatant nationality."

A flash of fright jabbed in my belly – I winced. Linda paled.

Akhmatov continued: "You just got two tickets on the *Sovremennyy*. We have to observe proper procedures before taking civilians on board." The left corner of his mouth rose: a tiny wry smile.

Linda straightened her back, while I exhaled slowly. *He tested us there, but did we fail or pass?* I thought.

"Miss Connor, you're a mechanic and the engine section has suffered casualties so they would need your hands." Akhmatov sounded like he was issuing an order.

Linda nodded.

Akhmatov looked at me: "Mr Bornewald, from what you have said, I believe that you know how to handle radios."

The ironies of life: I was about to work for Sweden's worst enemy. If Linda and I had not been in mortal danger, I would have responded with a bitter laugh. Instead my phony smile implied that serving the tsar was the right thing to do. "Yes, major."

"Good. You'll assist our signals officer. But right now I want a detailed description of the people that seized the mine. Any questions?" Akhmatov sounded as if he expected none.

I looked at Linda and she looked back, her face somewhat relaxed. She shook her head.

"No, major," I said.

"Good. Let's get started," said Akhmatov.

CHAPTER 8

The *Sovremennyy* departed at dusk. During the afternoon, a thick layer of low-altitude clouds from the north had gradually covered the sky. This was to our advantage, because the vehicle's smoke plume would now fade into the clouds at one thousand feet, thereby reducing the distance at which we could be spotted.

A military juggernaut is as cramped as a cloudship but with many more metal protrusions. If you don't learn to duck, your skin will soon be flecked with bruises. The crew wore sturdy leather jackets and helmets for protection. There were people everywhere and bunks were tucked away in unexpected locations. I was used to this kind of confined accommodation, but this vessel also reeked of sweaty men in poorly ventilated spaces. The noise was far worse than in a civilian cloudship, too. The rhythmic low-frequency clatter from the engine permeated every part of the juggernaut, as well as never-ending murmuring and wheezing in the tubing. At many stations, the crewmen used ear protection and communicated by sign language.

Linda and I rested side by side in narrow bunks on top of a storage compartment for spare parts. During the afternoon, I had repaired radio equipment on the bridge. It had suffered a bad hit during yesterday's clash. I had replaced parts of the electronics, rerouted cables and cleared the communications cubbyhole of shrapnel. At the same time, Linda had been assigned to the team that worked on the steam system.

My sleep was restless with colourful dreams that sent me back to the city of my youth. The disconnected sequences mixed childhood and adolescence and twisted perspectives and emotions.

Suddenly I, once again sixteen years old, hear my sister's screams and I run on paths with clumps of grass in the cracked soil through the shadows of spruces. Jackdaws caw above me and I know I will be too late. Suddenly I am inside a ruined barn with a smoking revolver in my right hand. A shaggy marauder squirms in pain on the ground, slowly bleeding to death. My sister's motionless body lies next to him. The marauder changes shape to a Juliusburgian soldier in white with a crushed rib cage.

I woke with a shout in a rumbling cubbyhole with a steel bulkhead fifteen inches above my face. One or two seconds passed before I recalled where I was. Linda slept soundly besides me, being more used to the noise. An hour passed before my anxiety receded and I returned to sleep.

Rays from the dawning sun reached across the bridge and touched the radio equipment in front of me. I sipped tea, feeling stiff, tired and nervous. The earphones pressed against my skull and filled my ears with ether cracklings. I slowly scanned the short-wave band in search of comprehensible broadcasts, mainly to give the impression that I was doing a serious effort.

One frequency carried audible dash-dot signals, but when I jotted them down, it was only random letters. I put the measurements of the directional aerial on an ice chart. The resulting line passed close to Juliusburg so it ought to be enciphered military traffic.

"Good morning, Mr Bornewald," said Akhmatov behind my back. He had sneaked up on me with a sound.

"G'd morn'" I mumbled.

"I'm here to relieve you," he said.

"Thanks, major." I removed the earphones and rotated the chair so I could get out of the cubbyhole.

Akhmatov looked pale and dishevelled. "Anything to report?" he said while getting seated.

"No news," I said and walked to the side of the bridge to look at the world around us: a flat, white, lifeless cosmos. Grey clouds covered the sky in all directions.

A voice behind my back bellowed: "Avrál!" – the Russian call for battle stations. A flurry of movements back and forth on the bridge, followed by shouted reports. I donned my helmet and stayed out of the way. The *Sovremennyy's* commander, lieutenant-colonel Volkov, came out of the captain's cabin next to the communications cubbyhole. He was still buttoning his leather jacket when he got into the commander's seat in the middle of the bridge.

The executive officer addressed me in German: "Mein Herr, Gefechtsstationen. Possible enemies at five o'clock. Assist major Akhmatov."

However, Akhmatov just waved me away. I found a quiet corner on the starboard side of the bridge, where I waited for new instructions. Looking abaft over the ice, I glimpsed two distant smoke plumes.

Volkov issued a string of orders. The rhythm of the engines quickened as the *Sovremennyy* accelerated and her three functioning main turrets rotated to point their guns at the presumed enemies.

The bridge was one of the least armoured parts of the juggernaut because of its many panoramic glass panes. I thought of yesterday's grisly cleaning of the communications cubbyhole and hoped that Linda was in a safer place in the vehicle's bowels.

A lieutenant with a field-glass pushed me out of the nook. Akhmatov was busy clicking the signalling key. He shouted a brief statement at Volkov, who responded with: *"Da,"* and issued another string of orders. A soldier started lowering steel shutters in front of several bridge windows.

I recalled the old military maxim war consists of ninety percent boredom and ten percent agony, filled my cup with tea from the nearest vacuum flask, and tried to summon some philosophical equanimity while the race over the ice continued. I failed.

The juggernaut's engines reverberated at maximum power and the hull creaked under ensuing strain. The long studs of the steel wheels tore chunks out of the ice sheet as the *Sovremennyy* rushed forward. The pursuers still gained on us. My binocular showed two long and sleek juggernauts, smaller than the *Sovremennyy* and each with only two main gun turrets. Two sudden flashes of light from the foremost enemy – instinctively I crouched.

A nearby thunderclap followed by steel shrapnel and ice fragments rattling against the *Sovremennyy's* port side. The unprotected glass panes on the bridge's port side suddenly sported constellations of pockmarks, but they did not shatter. No second explosion – that shell must have been a dud.

Thunder rolled through the vehicle when the *Sovremennyy's* three main guns fired a salvo. I rose and looked for the pursuers. Three blasts of ice shards surrounded the leading juggernaut, but she maintained her course and speed. A triple miss.

The *Sovremennyy's* secondary armament rattled, small-calibre auto-cannons that put strings of shells in an arc between us and the enemies. Thick smoke billowed from the impacts in the ice – an opaque screen that provided temporary concealment.

Volkov issued an order to the helmsman, who rotated the steering-wheel clockwise with great force. The *Sovremennyy* turned starboard with a harsh screech. The manoeuvre increased her angular velocity vis-à-vis the pursuers, which ought to reduce the risk of being hit.

The smokescreen obscured us for about twenty seconds, after which the enemy juggernauts came into view once again. Their column had also made a starboard turn, so their commander had assessed Volkov's intentions correctly. Meanwhile the *Sovremennyy* continued turning. I instinctively grabbed the nearest firm support. The *Sovremennyy's* guns thundered first. Two projectiles struck the foremost pursuer, whose silhouette disappeared behind flames and smoke. The third grenade exploded in the ice. The rear pursuer's two heavy guns flashed.

It sounded like a brigade of blacksmiths slammed their hammers all over the *Sovremennyy*. Two sharp flashes momentarily illuminated the interior of the bridge. The juggernaut tilted forward to the starboard in a convulsion that tossed me in an adjacent officer who lost his footing and fell. Panic-stricken I held on to the nearest porthole handle and struggled to stay on my feet. Loud screeching of metal against ice filled my ears. Something struck my back with a force that pressed the air out of my lungs.

When the *Sovremennyy* had lost all speed, two of her main guns fired. Half a second later, an enemy projectile crashed through the hull near the stern. An enormous double blast followed and the vehicle shook from one end to the other: a magazine explosion. The juggernaut's death throes knocked me down. My left elbow slammed into the deck and I screamed with pain.

Crack! A small-calibre armour-piercing projectile burst through a metal shutter and sprayed glass shards and steel splinters across the bridge. Something struck my chest near the heart. My eyesight flickered.

My eyes started working normally. The screams of the wounded drowned the hissing in my ears. I lay on my right side and saw a man eight inches away. His head, covered by a helmet, was twisted in an unnatural angle. My left armpit felt sticky. Pain pulsated in the muscle next to my left nipple – a long glass shard extended through my coat.

I pushed at the deck and got into an awkward sitting position, grimacing with pain at every move. Icy air leaked through the tears in my clothes. The battle seemed to be over. I looked around. The men that still were on their feet were busy saving wounded comrades' lives. The second hand on the bridge clock still moved even though the glass cover had been cracked.

Akhmatov appeared at my side with a medikit. He was dirty but seemingly without injuries. "Bornewald, how are you?"

"I don't know." My voice was barely audible.

"Lay down and I'll check you."

I rolled onto my back and looked at the ceiling. A huge red blotch caught my eyes. *What could have caused that?*

Akhmatov's hands moved along my torso and arms. "Nothing seems broken, but you are badly bruised. Now I'll remove the shard." He unbuttoned my clothes. A giant icy hand grasped my ribcage. Akhmatov pulled out the shard and smeared carbolic acid on the wound. A fierce burning sensation on top of the pain. My teeth gnashed when I clenched the jaws and stifled a scream. Akhmatov closed the wound with band-aids and buttoned my clothes.

"Make sure that a corpsman puts some stiches in that gash later today. Anyhow, you'll get an ugly scar. Maybe something to show Miss Connor. Now, remain on the deck for a while." Akhmatov moved to another wounded man.

I continued to look at the red blotch. My hands and feet trembled. My thoughts were chaotic, but I guessed that I had been knocked out for less than a minute. Cold gusts of wind danced through the bridge. The steam system wheezed and howled as it struggled with broken tubes. A thumping noise from below indicated that at least one engine was running – the *Sovremennyy* was not yet dead.

One thought burned in my mind: *What has happened to Linda?*

CHAPTER 9

The funeral service ended with the chaplain's mournful chant in Church Slavonic. The crewmen, wearing white polar uniforms and standing in formation, crossed themselves. Linda, standing at my side, did likewise, but I refrained; it is not a Wesleyan custom. My chest ached and it was hard stand in attention.

"Ave Maria, Mater Dei, ora pro nobis peccatoribus, nunc et in hora mortis nostrae," Linda whispered.

Lieutenant-colonel Volkov had ordered the crew to assemble on the lee side of the broken juggernaut. The men had erected a cairn of steel debris and ice blocks for the fallen and it looked like it would stand here forever. Beyond it, the glittering plain stretched to the horizon, where white met blue in a long straight line. The sun was behind us so the *Sovremennyy's* wreck cast a jagged shadow over the ceremony.

Looking to our right, I saw the smoke from the burning enemy juggernauts some miles away and thought: *Do they also bury their dead now?* We ignored them as they ignored us – a tacit armistice. It was obvious why, because the survivors had enough troubles as it was.

To our left, a row of lanky white iceboats waited for their passengers. They had been folded and stored inside the *Sovremennyy* – her equivalent of lifeboats. Several had been ruined during the battle, but enough remained in working condition to carry all survivors.

The funeral ended and the sergeants dismissed the men, who returned to work. Linda and I had no assignments for the time being so we headed for the medical station in a white tent on the lee side of the wreck. I wanted a corpsman to do something with my wound and after that I would get hold of a clean shirt and stitch the gash in my jacket.

"How are you doing?" I asked her.

She had been battered by a violent fall in the engine room when the *Sovremennyy* toppled, but at least she had suffered no cracked bones or deep cuts. "I can walk," she said, "but I can't run."

"My radio is broken. Can't be repaired. We're cut off from Leclerc." I shivered. *If we die out here, nobody will ever hear of our fate.* "The rest of my gadgets seem to have survived, but I haven't been able to test them."

"Kčortu! It only gets worse," Linda grunted.

The engine throbbed and the ventilation fan hummed as it pushed a stream of warm air onto my knees. The snowmobile's interior smelled of grease. I sat comfortably astride the pillion and looked straight south over Linda's shoulder. The ice sheet was flat, entirely without distinguishing landmarks. When she twisted the accelerator with her right hand, the engine responded properly. The pillion shifted slightly as Linda moved on the saddle.

I turned my head to the left to check the other snowmobile that Akhmatov drove alone. If one vehicle broke down, the other would be able to carry three passengers but not four. He looked back and Linda gave him a thumbs-up. He nodded and drove off, being the only one who knew the location of our destination. Our vehicle felt sluggish when Linda accelerated to fall in behind him; after all, it towed a sled with a fuel barrel and extra equipment.

I looked in the rear-view mirror: white sails burst like flowers from the masts of the ice boats, parked in two straight lines next to the *Sovremennyy*. The symmetry dissolved when the vessels started moving forward, leaning slightly away from the wind. They headed elsewhere and I presumed that I would never see them again.

I hummed for myself while the snowmobiles cut fresh tracks through the snow. Since departure Linda had stayed a steady thirty yards to Akhmatov's snowmobile. The sun now approached the western horizon. Maxidin pills kept us alert during the tedious hours.

"I don't trust that chap. He is too self-confident," Linda said breaking the silence for the first time since our departure.

"So ... but why?" My thoughts had wandered off to faraway lands because of the monotony and it took me a moment to respond.

"He's so bloody sure that we'll find some leviathan hunters at that islet, but why the hell would they sit there like a herd of defenceless mlatsy. All sensible ursines within a thousand miles got out of harm's way as soon as they heard about the war on the radio. I know how they think and I know what beasts lurk in the Juliusburg military." Linda's voice got shriller as she spoke. The horrors of the last few days had strained both of us badly and it sounded like Linda was approaching her breaking point.

"Well, military people often get involved in conspiracies. Maybe those hunters have cut a deal with Novgorod. After all, everyone around here seems to hate Juliusburg," I said.

"Kčortu! We should have refused to work with him," she said.

"We had no alternatives, did we? He knew what he wanted to do and what people he wanted to come along. Anyhow, we're heading away from the war, aren't we?" I said.

"Johnny, this is too much."

Her words surprised me. I searched for something sensible to say, but failed. "Together... together... we'll make it."

We drove through the night on a straight course. Dawn came, beaming gentle orange light across the ice and snow. Far ahead, almost where the ice met the sky, I glimpsed a darker dot. "Land ahoy," I said.

Linda said: "That's just a peak puncturing the ice sheet. It's like a tiny island."

"Have you been here before?" I said.

"No, but there are plenty of them and most of them look alike," she said.

This one may have looked like other from the outside, but it turned out to be something else. Akhmatov ended this stage of our journey by halting next to it. We unloaded the backpacks and other essential equipment after which Akhmatov disabled the steering of his snowmobile, filled its tank, started its engine and sent it away across the ice to create misleading tracks for any airborne pursuers. Then he covered the remaining vehicles with white tarpaulins taken from his sled.

When that job was completed, he guided us between rocks and boulders to a place near the islet's peak in the shadow of two crags. He rolled aside a small boulder and uncovered an uneven hole in the ground, less than three feet in diameter. "Ladies first," he said. "Light the kerosene lamp when you reach the bottom. It's in a niche to your right. Wait there for the luggage to come down. Mr Bornewald, stop halfway and pass the packs down from me to Miss Connor."

Linda descended with the help of footholds carved into the granite and disappeared out of sight. I followed her and, after we had handled the luggage, I continued to the bottom. Akhmatov stopped on the way down and I heard a few thuds when he covered the opening with the boulder.

Almost ten yards below ground I reached a flat stone floor. The faint light from the kerosene lamp illuminated a man-made cavern, about 25 by

25 feet. No ursine would ever be able enter this hideout; it had been made by humans for humans. The air was surprisingly warm, perhaps +10°C. An enclosed heating stove of unknown design, painted in red, occupied the middle of the room. Four metal bunk beds with mattresses and folded bed-linen stood along one wall. A primitive kitchenette in a corner had been stocked with canned food.

"The Novgorod military seems to have made a lot of preparations," I said.

"We've expected war for years," said Akhmatov as he removed his arctic clothing. His face was grey and haggard. "Let's sleep, all of us. We'll be safe here for a while. Soon we'll be seeing friends." He crawled into a bottom bunk, unfolded a wool blanket and fell asleep straight away.

Linda mumbled: "Sleep well," and climbed into a top bunk. I extinguished the kerosene lamp and got into bed, too.

The aroma of hot soup and coffee filled my nose. I opened my eyes and saw the rock chamber illuminated by the kerosene lamp. Akhmatov was busy making breakfast in the kitchenette across the room. His face had regained some colour since yesterday.

"Did you sleep well?" he asked.

"Yes, and I'm hungry," I said and got into a sitting position. My chest wound ached and my body was stiff. My wristwatch claimed that it was afternoon in the world above us, but my mind had a hard time accepting that. Judging from Linda's soft breathing, she was still asleep in the bunk above me.

"Soup is ready. Pork and vegetables," said Akhmatov and handed me a half-full steaming Bakelite guksi bowl.

The soup was bland and the coffee weak, but it did not matter – they quenched my hunger and thirst.

Some minutes passed before Akhmatov, still being busy in the kitchenette, broke the silence: "Mr Bornewald, I think that you haven't been truthful to me. Who are you?" He turned around and looked into my eyes.

The coffee mug trembled for a moment in my hand. "Do you want to see my Dutch passport?"

"Passports are easy to forge. And I actually believe that yours is genuine. However, your backpack contains things that no Dutch cloudman should possess. That binocular, for instance. I haven't seen anything like it before."

I remained silent to gather my thoughts. I had to make up an explanation that would sound credible to a Russian intelligence officer. "I'm a Dutch spy, working for the Inlichtingendienst. My mission is to monitor Alban developments that affect the interests of our realm."

"The Netherlands is a petty country at the fringe of the worst war in Europe for fifty years. What's your interest in Alba? Why do you carry so many strange gadgets?" Akhmatov's calm voice made me shiver.

"We depend on international trade. You may grumble about our wheeling and dealing with the Habsburg Empire, Russia and the republics at the same time, but we have to. Our cloudships and merchantmen travel all over the globe, you know that. I work alone in a hostile environment so I've got equipment to aid me. That binocular is a cutting-edge design from Carl Zeiss in Duisburg," I said.

"It looks like something out of a French adventure movie. And it has no Zeiss markings," said Akhmatov.

"That red stove over there is a sophisticated device. I don't understand how it can stay functional for so long periods without supervision," I said.

"Nor do I. But it has been built by Russia's foremost savants. Not by a pipsqueak state like the Netherlands." Akhmatov advanced toward me with a kitchen knife in his hand, his face expressionless. I scurried out of the bunk, getting ready for a brawl that I knew I would lose.

Suddenly Akhmatov's head jerked aside and he gasped with pain. A slim knife protruded from right side of his neck. He dropped his weapon and grasped for the knife's handle while blood splattered the floor around him.

I stepped forward and kicked at his right knee. He dodged by staggering backward while he waved his arms at me. A second knife hit his shoulder. I stopped for a moment. Akhmatov sat down with a thump and once again reached for his neck. I used the brief opening to kick him in the chest with great force. His torso fell backward and his skull slammed into the stone floor. He shivered for an instant and lay still.

Dead? Yes, my fingers confirmed that he had no pulse. I backed off and checked the room.

Linda squatted in her bunk with a third throwing knife ready. "Johnny, are you okay?"

I sat down in my bunk. The hands trembled uncontrollably. "Yes," I whispered. "You saved my life."

Linda got down and sat next to me. Her face was stiff and pale.

"You're an ace," I continued.

"That's necessary for a plebeian woman fighting in this war, isn't it?" Her voice was flat.

"That's why you're a rebel?" I asked.

"I don't want to be a third-class citizen: woman and riffraff. Do you understand that?" she said.

"Yes, I do. Look at the colour of my skin." I did not have the mental energy to continue the conversation, so I got up, dragged the corpse into a corner and covered it with blankets. Meanwhile Linda wiped the floor with a towel. When I checked my backpack, I saw that Akhmatov had not damaged any device during his inspection.

I decided to inspect the strange stove. It was completely enclosed by a metal casing and appeared to work without combustion. A yellow band of stencilled Cyrillic letters ran along one side with the words Опасность для жизни in a larger font than the rest. "Linda, what does this say?" I pointed at the text.

Linda squatted next to the stove and translated: "Mortal danger! This unit contains substances that emit ionizing radiation. This unit may only be disassembled by certified personnel. Covering the unit's exterior may cause fire. Date of assembly: 27 November 1936. To be decommissioned: 27 November 1946." She looked at me. "Do you understand this?"

"Yes. Have you heard of ionizing radiation?" I said.

"No."

"There are elements that are naturally unstable. Their atoms break apart and turn into other elements while emitting invisible particles or rays. It is called 'atomic decay' and it can be harmful to living tissue," I said.

"I learned in school that atoms are indivisible," she said.

"Well, some physicists have discovered that nature is more complex than that," I said. "Anyhow, certain of those elements become warm during decay and this stove apparently uses that property to produce heat for years. I had no idea that was possible, but I'm no physicist. And I did not know that Russia had reached so far in this field."

Linda moved to a bunk and motioned me to sit next to her. "How come you know so much about this?"

"Do you know who Alfred Nobel was?" I said.

"The man who invented dynamite?" said Linda.

"That's right. Towards the end of his life, he resided in one of the Italian states. The Pan-European war in the 1890s shattered his trust in the existing societies. He was rich and without heirs, so he willed his wealth to the establishment of the Nobel Institute, an independent foundation that is charged with furthering peace through science. That's my employer. Nobel specified that the institute would reside in Hamburg, an independent city state that he thought was peaceful. The institute has recruited many brilliant physicists: Danish Niels Bohr, Swiss Albert Einstein, Lise Meitner and Leo Szilard from the Habsburg Empire. Their ideas about the inner nature of matter are revolutionary," I said.

"I've never heard of that, but I've only been to primary school," said Linda.

"The institute is discreet. We're in the middle of a war," I said. "Anyhow, now I have proof that the Russians have known about decaying elements for more than four years and I must report that to the institute."

"Easier said than done." Linda was quiet for a while. "Do you have colleagues in Alba, people that can help us?"

"Yes, but I need a radio transmitter to reach them," I said.

Linda switched subject: "Yesterday, Akhmatov disposed of one snowmobile for a diversion. He didn't worry about retaining only one here."

I nodded: "He must have known something we're ignorant of." My eyes checked the cavern but found nothing unexpected.

"This islet contains a means of escape." Linda sounded certain.

"I think you're right." I switched subject to something that had troubled my minds for some days. "How come a company director picks a fight with Russia?"

"The Rhodes conglomerate behaves like a country here in Alba, even though they pay lip service to the Orange State."

"I know little of what's going on in Africa, but quarrelling with the tsar? Terboven must have some cards up his sleeve if he thinks that his organization can prevail against Russia in the long run," I said.

"Do you have any ideas?" asked Linda.

I shook my head. "No, nothing more than it must be an ace. And that's scary."

Linda and I spent a second night in the cavern to restore our vigour, but we agreed that we had to depart after that because soon Akhmatov's corpse would start to stink and we were not able to hoist it safely to the surface with available equipment. Back injuries would be disastrous to our continued journey.

After breakfasting on Russian canned food, we climbed to the surface. The world remained as it had been: a rock islet in a white infinity. Grey clouds raced across the sky, riding on a biting wind from the north-east.

"There ought to be another hideout," insisted Linda. She was right, but we had to search for many cold hours to find it. When she twisted a certain boulder next to the ice sheet, she was able to topple it and uncover a deep and narrow unheated cavity cluttered with machinery. We found several long sheets and rods of metal and beyond them we saw a simple engine, six studded steel wheels and some fuel barrels.

Linda got the picture at once: "A dismantled ice-buggy." She displayed her skill as a mechanic by reassembling it in an hour.

When she was done, I asked: "Where are we going next?"

"After our arrival Akhmatov said: 'Soon we'll be seeing friends.' We'll have to look for clues in his belongings," she said.

We returned to the warm cavern and searched Akhmatov's possessions and clothes. Linda struck gold when she opened a small notebook and found a crude hand-drawn map with three scribbled notations for latitudes and longitudes. I used a sextant and my wristwatch to determine our current position. It matched one of Akhmatov's positions, whereas the other two were to our north.

"Let's head for the nearest one, shall we?" said Linda.

"Yes," I said.

"It'll be a long journey. Do we have enough Maxidin pills?" she asked.

"Sure, let's get moving at once." *That drug will be my death soon*, I thought.

CHAPTER 10

A long ice-buggy journey is more tedious than you would expect. You are coped up close to the ice in a cramped and noisy cabin. Initially you may feel adventurous as you dash ahead, but after a few hours you feel only stiff and bored. The landscape never changes, except for occasional grey peaks penetrating the ice. Linda drove the craft expertly and I had no wish to relieve her. The Maxidin kept us awake during one day and one night as we covered almost 700 miles at an average speed of about 30 knots. We took only a few brief breaks for meals and position checks, because we wanted to get out the war zone as quickly as possible. My memories of that journey deal mainly with enforced immobility and never-ending aches. A large dose of alertness drugs does strange things to the mind.

Soon after dawn our destination appeared as a tiny jag at the horizon. As we approached, it grew into hills and crags that I scrutinized through my binocular. A surprising amount of brown-grey rock protruded through ice and snow and plume of steam or smoke rose from several locations. I twisted the zoom control and my vision jumped forward. A pennant in green and black fluttered from a hundred-foot metal pole. I described for it Linda.

"Ursine haven. Lucky we're." Her muddled speech was a side effect of the Maxidin.

"What?" I said.

"A meeting place, warm, a peace place, rest, a stop." She looked at me. "What say I?"

"You're dazed. It will pass as the drug leaves your body," I said.

An ursine haven, such as this place called Gishtir, is best compared to an oriental caravanserai. Gishtir had been established long ago in this place where hot springs caused by volcanism penetrated the bedrock. It consisted of a maze of interconnected low round stone buildings. Its interior was as humid as a rain forest, but with an ever-present odour of sulphur. Many trade routes met here and therefore there was a need for a neutral meeting ground where public display of weapons was banned, that is, a good place for Akhmatov "to meet friends".

When we entered Gishtir's spacious interior, I saw no other humans, something that I appreciated under our current circumstances. However, such travellers must visit the place every now and then because the superintendent, a scarred old ursine with a maimed right hand, provided two proper beds for the plain room that Linda rented. She communicated with him in a Lingua Franca used by ursine traders and we got what we needed at a reasonable price. Soon we collapsed in those beds and vanished into the realm of sleep.

I opened my eyes and looked at the grey ceiling above my bed, feeling that I once again was able to think clearly.

Three days had rushed by in a jumble of dizzy spells, meals and irregular sleep. Our sleeping patterns had been out of synch, so I had spent most of my waking hours in silence. The superintendent had sent three meals a days to our door: bland but filling dishes that suited the human stomach.

Linda huddled on her bed, wrapped in a blanket. She looked at me with clear eyes. "Good morning."

"Good morning," I said. "I stink. I must have a bath and wash my clothes." I worried that my shoulder wound would get infected.

"Me too. Also, my period has started so I feel sick," she said.

"Any bath facility in this place?" I asked.

"Sure, but you'll have to share it with the ursines," she said. "I'll order a tub so I can take care of myself in here."

The thermae was a vast building by itself, partially cut into the bedrock, with two hot springs in the floor. Their sulphuric tang, mixed with the nutmeg odour of wet ursines, permeated the hall. Sturdy servants carried buckets from those wells to a double semicircle of brass bath tubs.

I cleaned my wound carefully with a coarse soap and checked that it was healing as it should. While a washer took care of my dirty clothes, I slid into the warm water and let it soften my aching muscles. A human is notable smaller than an ursine so I floated comfortably in the tub. I wanted to analyse what had happened to us and the best way was to relax and let my thoughts wander freely. Bulky ursines scrubbed their fur is the surrounding tubs while chatting and joking with each other. They paid no heed to me and their voices turned into background buzz.

A few new facts carried immediate importance for my work at the Nobel Institute. First, Terboven trusted that the Rhodes conglomerate was able to challenge Russia in Alba and get away with it in the long term. Even though Russia currently used her military to subjugate Scandinavia and prevent the republican rebellion from spreading into her lands, sooner or later those conflicts would end. And then common sense said that the conglomerate bosses would have to answer to the tsar. However, Terboven obviously believed that he could avoid that fate and I needed to figure out why he thought so.

Second, the Russian military had developed new ways of using radioactive substances, something that we at the Institute so far had thought was our secret. For the last two hundred years, we westerners have tended to see Russia as an empire mismanaged by self-indulgent aristocrats. But that was no longer the case. More than four years ago Russian scientists had developed a technology that might be used for city-wrecking weapons. Terboven ought to be ignorant of that, because if we had not known, how could he? Once again, the institute needed to find out more of what was going on, but how would it be possible to peek into Russia's secret files?

"Johnny, what's keeps you moving … in your heart?" Linda asked when we shared dinner in our room that evening.

I put down the spoon in the bowl of bitter stew and looked her in the eyes. "Why do you want to know that?" It would not be easy to answer her question.

"You're a scholar but you live like a rootless wanderer year after year. Not even the ursine nomads are as solitary as you. I can't understand why you do that to yourself," she said.

My gaze flittered around the dining hall. It was an open space because ursines customarily eat standing or moving around. We sat in a corner on a woven rug with food bowls on the floor around us. My back rested against the stone wall while Linda sat cross-legged in front of me. A dozen ursines ambled in the hall, occasionally glancing in our direction but otherwise leaving us alone.

When I had gathered my thoughts, I responded: "I have nothing to return to. The tsar's secret police would arrest me at once. If I escaped the hangman's noose, I would be banished to a Siberian penal colony."

"If you want to hide from the Okhrana, why don't you just vanish into Magalhana's highlands?"

"True," I said. I hesitated for a moment. Speaking of my youth was never pleasant. "But running away wouldn't suffice in my heart. When I was an adolescent, I got hold of banned books written by men like Karl Staaf, John Wesley and Benedetto Croce. I started to dream of a better society, in which the hungry will get bread instead of lashings. I became a republican activist to work for that end."

"I've never heard of those men. Please, tell me more," said Linda.

"A thousand years ago, my father's ancestors said that 'power resides in the spear point'. The issue is then: 'who holds the spear and where does he point it?'" I started to expound on freedom and equality for everyone.

Eventually Linda said: "Stop it, Johnny. Enough for today."

I closed my mouth. I had used the opportunity to say speak about all that burned in my mind. Linda lay down on her bed with the hands behind the head and closed her eyes. I reached for my water cup to moisten my dry throat.

"Do you think all that really is possible?" said Linda.

"They didn't build Rome in one day. If enough people choose to go in the same direction, they can work miracles. That is the goal of your rebellion and mine. I am responsible to God and my conscience for my choice. I know my road and that gives me strength."

Linda opened her eyes. "You've received a lot for free. People like me haven't. Our goals are less ambitious."

"But I've lost almost all of my privileges," I said. "But a few things can't be taken away. A solid education has given me a clear sight. My father taught me to assume responsibility and do my duty. My elder brother showed me the difference between good and bad duties. So I decided to put my talents to service of the downtrodden."

"Do you think that ursines should have the same rights, the same opportunities, too?" she asked.

"Yes, all intelligent beings are equal. The same rules should apply all over the world, regardless of your species," I said.

Linda shook her head. "There are plenty of humans in Alba who think that such ideas are nonsense. You don't know the ursines. They don't think like we do."

"Does it matter? They, too, have souls."

CHAPTER 11

For almost two weeks we mostly slept, ate and talked. The journey from Fredriksborg to Gishtir had taken about the same amount of time. After ten days in the haven, we had regained enough strength to start planning for the next stage of journey, going back to Acheron.

A caravanserai provides many advantages for a person who wants to keep a low profile. All visitors are passers-by, each with his worries. In the common areas you chat about the weather, hear people's tall tales and listen to the natives' screechy music, but nobody is nosy. We did not encounter anyone that we could associate with Akhmatov. His plans might have gone awry because of the war or we might have chosen the wrong destination.

Linda listened for news from the war. Newly-arrived ursines spoke of clashes here and there, but it was hard to get a comprehensive picture – too many rumours, too much speculation. Several Russian outposts appeared to have been attacked, sometimes successfully, sometimes not, but it was impossible to figure how big forces had been involved. However, it was clear that the Russians currently were on the defensive, but that was no surprise. In most of their wars during the last two centuries, they usually had fared badly in the beginning, but when they had assembled a numerical superiority they had taken the war to enemy. In the beginning of the Swedish rebellion, it had looked like the freedom fighters would prevail, but eventually the Russians gained the upper hand.

Linda was able to make a travel plan with hand-drawn maps from what she found in Gishtir's small collections of books and from documents shown to her by ursine travellers. These fellows made good impressions, composed and courageous people who knew everything about the ice sheet.

Many spoke comprehensible English or German. They were willing provide tips and advice, because they knew it was a matter of life and death.

On the twelfth day in Gishtir, we compiled a final travel plan: we would head for Zilwerstaad, an outpost controlled by Juliusburg. Our cover story: we were survivors from a civilian juggernaut that had been shot to pieces on the ice sheet by an unidentified military juggernaut.

In war plans rarely survive the first contact with reality. During the night between the twelfth and the thirteenth day that reality caught up with us.

Loud knocks of the door tore me out of deep sleep. Several seconds passed before I had gathered my wits and was able to act. Linda looked equally dazed when she sat up in her bed. I grabbed my electric torch from under my pillow.

Someone started to hammer the door with a fist. "Nister Ghorneraltt, wake ukk! I need to talk to you." The hoarse bass voice that could not pronounce B, M, and P indicated that the speaker was an ursine male with a poor knowledge of English

I slid out the warmth of the blankets, put the feet in my boots to shield them from the cold floor, and pulled the door two inches ajar with the safety chain in place. My electric torch revealed a huge dark furry face with hard green eyes and the ursines' cleft upper lip. Polar goggles rested on his forehead. My nose burned from the acrid stench of the grease that ursines smear into the fur to improve its wind protection factor. Two large-calibre Steyr revolvers and three ursine blades dangled from his belt.

This bodes ill, I thought. "Sir, who are you?"

"My name is Vüdras and I carry some important matters to you on my back," the ursine said.

He must be using some native idiom, I thought. "I'm listening."

"Not here. Let me in so that we can speak packlessly," he said.

"No armed strangers in my room," I said.

"Kshrêgith!" he rumbled and stomped three feet at the same time. "No time for bickering. Human enemies approaching. We must talk now. Otherwise too late for all.

I backed into the room. "We're in a haven."

"I think soldiers of the rising sun care little for our customs. I know their ways. They kill when they want," Vüdras said.

Japanese in Alba – they fight side by side with Juliusburg – now I understand. I remembered the newspaper reports about the Japanese army's brutal capture of Manila. Much had been written since the 1920s about Japan's wars of conquest in Asia, but so far they had stayed out of Alba. I shivered. "Why have you come for me?"

"Kheterly, man in white clothes, has sent me. You should know who he is," said Vüdras.

That must be Peter Lee, I thought and unlatched the security chain. "Please, come in."

Vüdras trotted into the room and turned around between our beds to face the door. Linda lit our oil lantern.

"What do you want?" I asked.

"Many hundred soldiers coming this way," he said

"I know how dangerous that army is. Why do you want to warn us?" I said.

"Kheterly wants you come with me and my braves to him. He needs your hands," Vüdras said.

I do not know the drunkard! I only met him during a journey, I thought. "Why would we help him?"

"As a favour for saving you from Japanese," said Vüdras.

"What kind of help does he need?" I said.

"He is badly hurt and need help from humans, help we cannot give," said Vüdras.

"You're too vague," I said.

"I don't know everything. Come now with me!" Once again, that triple stomp. "Just one night and day with our ice-buggy."

"That's far away," I said.

"Maybe, but safe from Japanese," he said.

"Why am I supposed to believe your story?" I said.

"Do as you wish. If you don't believe, soon you are dead – or prisoner," he said.

For Linda's sake I must comply. Peter Lee knows that, I thought. "We'll go with you. Give us a few minutes to pack."

While we were completing that task, I asked Linda whether she knew what clan Vüdras belonged to, but she had no idea. "He must be from some pretty faraway place," she explained.

Vüdras and his friends had alerted everybody. Visitors and staff were abandoning Gishtir in the dim light from torches and oil lamps. The Japanese would only find an empty shell. Ice-buggies departed in all directions while we were loading our belongings on Vüdras's vehicle and his friends, a dozen rough-looking black-furred ursines, were keeping a close watch on the surroundings.

The ensuing journey was as uncomfortable and monotonous as one could expect. The stench of unwashed ursines compounded the misery. I tried to map the course of the four ice-buggies in my head, but soon I concluded that the huge margin of error made the notion pointless.

We arrived at our destination after sunset: a tall craggy promontory rising from the ice sheet. The ice-buggies drove into a broad cavern. Its interior, lit by electrical lamps, stretched almost three hundred feet into the bedrock with most of the floor covered by ice. Two dozen ice-buggies were parked along the sides. The smoky air smelled of coal and grease. A squad of ursines trotted forward to welcome us. Two escorted Linda and me through winding warm passages to a small window-less room with two bunks and a hot meal on a low table. Their English was limited to phrases like "come along" and "rest here". We were too exhausted to care; we ate and fell asleep without even talking to one another.

"Welcome!" Peter Lee reclined on a bed with a mound of pillows behind the back and a brown blanket over the legs. "My apologies for not getting out of bed to greet you, but my leg is ruined." His face had turned gaunt and tired, his clothes were dirty and unkempt, but his eyes were still sharp. "Breakfast, perhaps?" He gestured toward a stone table with all sorts of ursine delicacies stacked on small plates. "Those sausages are spicy and tasty. There are stools for you behind the table."

We were fresh out of bed and Linda had to be as hungry as I was. "Ladies first," I said and she moved ahead.

Peter Lee's room was next to ours. There were no doors in this settlement – it seemed to be a human innovation that did not interest ursines – but a thick curtain covered the entry. We must be in a volcanic area, because the grey-brown rock was warm to the touch. Somebody had painted colourful naïve pictures of the sun and strange animals on the stone surface.

When Linda had filled her plate, I dealt with the buffet. Peter Lee must have eaten already, because he was merely sipping some hot fennel-smelling beverage from a clay cup. "I'll dispense with the introductory small talk, Miss Connor and Mr Bornewald, because we had enough of that on the *Lady Margaret*. Miss Connor, I think that you are the person you claim to be, but you, Mr Bornewald, are not."

I gazed at him while hiding the worries that raced through my mind behind a professional mask.

Peter Lee continued: "You see, an aristocrat will sooner or later reveal his true class because of his self-assured behaviour. Despite your middle-class disguise in the *Lady Margaret*, I noticed that you are from a more sophisticated milieu despite your dark skin. I am not such a drunkard that you might have come to believe." His voice reeked with smugness. "Small slips, like how you handle cutlery at a meal. You are not Dutch. You are an aristocrat from northern Germany or Scandinavia."

I did not respond.

"Who are you, Mr Bornewald? The truth, please," he said.

"Why would I answer that question?" I said to buy time. I hated that man for having forced us into his schemes.

"Lives are at stake now – yours, mine, and hers." He nodded toward Linda.

"You're obviously allied to a major ursine faction," I said to divert the conversation while I reviewed the new situation. "They picked us up in Gishtir at your orders. You're no ordinary scholar. Who are you? My question is as justified as yours."

"As justified? Well, I saved your lives in Gishtir. You owe me something in return," he said.

"You're surprisingly well-informed about our journey," I said.

"Correct, my ursine allies travel to many places. And when they return here, they report what they've seen and heard. A few days ago, some young braves came here after spending a night in Gishtir. They told me that they had seen two humans there and when I heard their descriptions I realized that it had to be you. That strengthened my suspicions that you are not what you claim. Mr Bornewald, you're at a significant disadvantage right now, but if you provide a satisfactory explanation for what you are up to, we might reach a mutually beneficial understanding. Please, no beating around the bush."

If he works for a monarch, Linda and I will end up with slit throats in a nearby crevasse. If he works for a republic, collaboration may be possible, I thought. "I don't serve the emperor, despite my aristocratic heritage," I said.

"Nor do I," said Lee. "We may be fellow travellers after all."

"Whose side do you support?" I said. *If he works for the rebellion, we have an unsavoury comrade-in-arms.*

"The ursines. The great powers have dealt harshly with the natives in Africa and Asia. I don't want that to happen in Alba, too," said Lee.

For Linda's safety, I must expose my best card, I thought. "I work for the Nobel Institute."

"I've heard of that. If you speak the truth, we would become co-belligerents opposing the same enemy. Can you prove it?" he said.

I went to fetch my backpack from our room and put a few devices on Peter Lee's brown blanket. He inspected them for a minute or two and handed them back. "I believe you. Only the boffins at Office Z design such stuff."

A chilling statement: Office Z was a top secret section that few outsiders had heard of. "Who is your superior?" I asked.

"I work for the University of Heidelberg and the republican government of Saxony. You'll have to take my word for it, because I have no proof," he said.

I did not care whether this was true or not, because I would not trust him under any circumstance until he had proved otherwise in action. "Why do you need our help?"

"My leg caught a bullet during my journey across Alba. I can't walk," he said.

"At New Bristol, right?" I said.

"How do you know?" Lee's voice turned sharp as a glass shard.

"I saw it from the observation tower. I had a binocular. There were two snipers, probably the Schnittkes," I explained.

Peter Lee sighed. "So, thanks for that piece of information. It won't help me, but at least I got my suspicions confirmed." He put his cup to the lips and took a large gulp. "The war has taken an unexpected turn. Japan has entered the fray as an ally to Juliusburg and landed a lot of troops in Alba. Also, in the northern hemisphere, her home fleet has attacked the Russian naval base at Port Arthur and her Korea army marches through Manchuria. Tokyo is fighting on the same side as the European republics."

So that's Terboven's hidden ace! I thought. The Japanese must have started planning years ago for this operation, because moving troops by air from northeast Asia to Alba require a lot of cloudships. The notion of Juliusburg and Japan fighting on our side revolted me. "If you want to help the ursines, your work is going get a lot harder now," I said. "The Japanese show no mercy. Remember Manila."

Peter Lee nodded. "Yes, we're in hurry if we want to nip this development in the bud."

That's impossible, I thought. "So what do you want to do?"

"You two are needed for something that no ursine can do. An expedition to our enemies' underground secrets," he said.

"Do we have the choice to abstain?" *Of course not, my question is a mere formality. That man considers us to be his tools, nothing else,* I thought.

"No." A single word with a dry bureaucratic sound. I expected something more and Lee delivered it after two or three silent seconds, "To late to back down. Now we'll drive together straight into Tartarus."

"Do you trust Lee?" whispered Linda. "I don't." She and I sat on my bed with our backs against the warm bedrock. We were waiting for a meeting with some ursine chieftains about Peter Lee's plans.

"A third-rate friend – the enemy of our enemies," I said. "You and I know what that is worth. But we're riding the tiger." My voice was low, too. "We've got to hang on to survive and jump away when the chance arrives."

Linda changed subject: "You – a republican aristocrat? I didn't know there were such people."

"But that's true. With a pompous surname and everything else. I come from Gothenburg in Sweden, though as a child I lived most of the time in Greifswald in Swedish Pomerania," I answered.

"How can a nobleman look the way you do?" she asked.

"Dark-skinned you mean? Well, my father travelled a lot when he was young, and my mother is from Danish East India."

An ursine voice from the corridor interrupted our conversation: "Nister Ghorneraltt, it is tine to sollow with ne."

At the rear of the hangar-like cavern in which we had arrived yesterday, the ursines had cut several smaller halls into the bedrock. One, with an ice-covered floor, served as our conference facility. Four European ice vehicles were parked in the middle with ample room around them. It appears that ursines want lots of space when they are indoors, a trait that probably is connected to their inability to stand still for more than a few seconds. During a meeting they walk back and forth and scan the surroundings, but they are still able to register what the speakers say. That habit annoyed me, but I just had to accept it.

Peter Lee waited for us, huddled under thick blankets in a primitive wheelchair. Its shape and proportions looked odd, so it had probably been built here. Four ursines ambled around him while a few others circled beyond them.

"My lady, sir, good day," Lee said in a formal manner with an awkward bow in our direction. Then he switched to an ursine language. He must have been in great pain, because every time he moved his face stiffened.

After a minute or so, he once again turned his attention to us and said in English: "These ursine gentlemen, Terakh, Trishkin, Khader and Rlishi, are high-ranking leaders among our allies." I bowed slightly in their direction and they responded by raising their arms. "They are about to hear my proposed action plan and approve it if they are satisfied. Before I start with that, I need to know whether either of you can handle a steam-powered snowcat."

"Yes," said Linda. "Are we talking about that one?" She pointed at a white-painted angular tracked vehicle with a tall slim smokestack. It was the size of a lorry, though without a flatbed, and its windows were protected by sturdy metal mesh.

"That's the one," said Lee.

"That's a Proteo 2G built in Turin, Italy in 1934. The engine provides about fifty horsepower, but you have shovel coal all the time. Is it is a good condition?" Linda directed the question at everyone present with the self-confidence of an expert.

"Yes, nadan." An ursine mechanic with oil stains along the arms did his best to speak English. "De haz dun a lot to retair it."

Linda switched to an ursine language and started a rapid conversation with the mechanic. After a few minutes she addressed Peter Lee in English: "Good that you have converted it to oil instead of coal. That electrical fuel pump will save me a lot of work. And there will be less smoke." She walked up the vehicle, opened its hood and started checking the machinery.

Meanwhile Lee addressed me: "Mr Bornewald, are you able to drive it, too?"

"Probably, but expect the trip to be a bit jerky," I said. Actually I felt more optimistic than I pretended.

Lee turned to the ursines. After talking with them for a few minutes, he interrupted Linda's inspection. "Miss Connor, Mr Bornewald, please come along to the order room."

That turned out to be a plain room with a blackboard and a stand for maps. Lee assumed command and switched between English and an ursine tongue during the lecture: "This is Post 14, a Russian outpost, located at a rock island." Lee's metal pointer touched a spot on a regional map of the ice sheet. "The ice runs almost all the way to the mountainside, just like here. The Russians have been working inside that peak for more than two hundred days. It took some time for their activities to catch our attention, but when our lads reported a visit by senior dignitaries from the tsar's colonial administration, we realized that something important is going on. There are caves inside and that is remarkable by itself. This is a bedrock mountain and caves don't form there through geological processes. Whatever the Russians have found, we'll deprive them of it. That's we need human participants, because ursines are not good at climbing vertical surfaces. My two allies will stand in for me, because my leg is a mess." Lee made a gesture in our direction.

I remembered what he had said earlier – *we can't say no* – and phrased my comment accordingly: "The Russians will hardly welcome us. How are we supposed to handle that?"

"Post 14 is lightly defended. The Russians don't want to attract attention and they are also short of troops in Alba, particularly after the Japanese intervention. Our ursine allies will attack with a clear numerical superiority and seize the place. Then we humans will enter it and uncover whatever is hidden there. Since I now have your assistance, Terakh, Trishkin, Khader and Rlishi have decided to approve of the raid." Lee sounded like a business manager instructing his staff.

"And if there will be fighting deep inside that mountain?" I said.

"We'll deal with such matters there and then, but I am sure that both Miss Connor and you know how to handle a rifle."

I nodded. Firefights in confined spaces are always deadly. I had not fired a gun for a long time, but no words from me would be able to make Lee revise his plans, so I stayed silent. That man held his abilities in too high esteem.

Lee and the ursines started to discuss tactical issues with the help of the blackboard. Linda did her best to make summarizing translations. The arrows drawn with chalks showed that the ursines understood the military problems they faced. These fellows were combat veterans, not reckless braves.

After the evening meal Linda and I huddled together on my bed in our room. It had been a strenuous day. After lunch, Lee had ordered us to prepare the Proteo for the raid and we had stowed fuel barrels, food and tools in its spacious cargo compartment. The wound in my chest ached after all the lifting.

"Lee deceives us." Linda's voice spewed venom. "His gestures and mimics stink of falsehood. There must be something big they want to pick up at Post 14, something so heavy that an ice-buggy can't carry it. That's why the need the Proteo. They have also put a strange rack on its roof." She caught her breath. "Do you think they'll shoot us when he doesn't need our arms and legs any longer?"

"Yes, they will," I said. "So we must make ourselves indispensable until we get a chance to run away."

CHAPTER 12

The following morning more than a hundred ursines swarmed into the huge cavern and manned two dozen ice-buggies. After ten minutes, the raid force departed from the promontory.

We humans shared the Proteo and took turns behind the wheel to drive around the clock. Peter Lee managed his driving duties by eating painkillers, but was too weak to do much else. Our speed was limited to fifteen knots so soon the ice-buggies disappeared ahead of us. However, we would follow a straight course to the assembly point, whereas they would disperse and approach it by roundabout routes. An ursine squadron moving in force across the ice might attract undesirable attention and even though the Russians had few aircraft in the region, it was important to reduce that risk.

Maxidin, monotony, noise: these three words summarize 36 hours' journey. The glare from sunlight on ice wore out the eyes, despite our sunglasses. We handled calls of nature in the cargo compartment behind the fuel barrels and we cooked food on a camping stove in the crew compartment. Every now and then I topped the fuel tank by pumping oil by hand from a barrel. We slept in shifts on a passenger couch behind the driver's seat.

At sunset the day after our departure we reached our destination, an anonymous spot on the ice sheet. Several ice-buggies had preceded us and more arrived from all corners of the compass during the next hour. When darkness had fallen, we had to exit our warm cabin to take Peter Lee to a staff meeting. A kicksled served as an improvised wheelchair and we pushed it to a huge white tent in the middle of the pack of ice vehicles.

Linda and I suffered from Maxidin hangovers and huddled at the rear of the tent while waiting for a chance to retire. The ursines did not stand still and their restless shuffling pressed us against the cold tent cover. The air was as thick with ursine odours as in Gishtir's thermae. Peter Lee made an apparently coherent review of the battle plan in an ursine language and Linda translated important bits into English. The braves saluted Lee by bellowing cheers when he had finished. Terakh was the next speaker and his words incited the braves to clamouring war dances where waving blades reflected the gleam of kerosene lanterns. Linda and I quickly retreated out into the cold to avoid being trampled.

A huge fan contraption rumbled beyond the ice-buggies, but I did not understand its purpose. After ten minutes we returned inside, where Terakh still spoke though the dancing had abated. Peter Lee slept sitting on the kicksled, so we took him back to the Proteo without anyone objecting. There we, too, went to sleep.

The sharp light of the rising sun penetrated my eyelids and jabbed a jolt of pain through my head. I sat up and realized that my eyes did not function properly. The hangover persisted – I was getting hooked on Maxidin. *If I get out of this mess alive, I mustn't touch that drug ever again*, I thought.

Outside the Proteo colossi had grown out of the ice. I struggled to make my eyes to regain focus and got tossed into a living nightmare: a dozen off-white hulks cast long shadows across our site. Their pulsating bodies shifted slightly back and forth. I recognized the Alban leviathans from book illustrations and now I understood their true size: living hills surrounded our camp.

Linda was still asleep whereas Peter Lee sat on the floor and gulped whisky straight out of a bottle. "I succeeded," he cried. "I managed to synthesize the right pheromones. Now I can send them wherever I want. Do you want a swig?" He waved the bottle in my direction.

"Hell no," I said. "I feel rotten. I need food." I rummaged through a carton of food before lighting the camping stove. I did not want to see that man, but there was no escaping him right now.

The greasy smells of cooking filled the compartment and woke Linda. She merely grunted while eating boiled sausages with stale bread and washing them down with fruit juice.

Food in the belly made life more bearable and lessened my headache. Peter Lee seemed to have gone off the tracks completely, his mind addled by a mix of alcohol, painkillers and Maxidin. *Well, hardly our problem*, I thought.

Linda and I ran a detailed checklist for the Proteo to ensure that it was ready for today's battle. While we were working, two ursines knocked on the door and called for something.

"They want Mr Lee," explained Linda.

"Let's give them what they ask for," I said. We dressed him for the Arctic cold and handed him over for transportation to the staff tent. I kept the whisky bottle because I wanted him to be able to speak.

A few minutes later, an ursine returned and called for us. "He wants us to join the staff meeting," said Linda.

In the big tent we found that the partially coherent Peter Lee reclined on a pile of skin rugs. An ursine stood behind him and made sure he did not fall over. A dozen others milled around the blackboard, on which Terakh had drawn a sketch map. He addressed Linda. "He wants to explain the battle plan for us so that we will ensure that Peter Lee's parts are executed properly," she explained.

I nodded and she started doing a simultaneous translation. Peter Lee looked at us every now and then during the briefing and towards the end he vomited on the ice. *He's going to hell quickly. If he dies before we're able to escape, we'll die, too,* I thought.

We returned to the Proteo ten-fifteen minutes later and discovered that ursine mechanics were putting rockets in the rack on the roof. When ready, they proceeded to bolt an unwieldy fan behind that rack. Linda and I got busy checking the new installations and making sure that the wiring was properly connected all the way to the driver's dashboard. The success of the operation, and our survival, depended on the equipment's flawless performance. Peter Lee would hardly be sober until late in the evening, so Linda and I had to manage everything.

When the mechanics had completed their assignments, Linda and I sat down in the drivers' seats and rehearsed dry runs of our tasks during the attack. That proved to be easier than we had expected. We even had got orders not to risk our lives, because Terakh wanted us to be alive and healthy for the post-assault investigation of Post 14.

One hour after dawn Linda started the Proteo and I activated the roof fans that spread pheromones all around us. The off-white hills started moving and the ursines scattered to avoid getting crushed.

The leviathan herd surrounded us in all directions and I could barely make out the horizon beyond the pulsating bodies. Linda increased the speed to 15 knots and the monsters had no problem keeping up with us. According to plan, the ursines' ice-buggies followed closely behind the herd.

If any leviathan decided to check our vehicle closely we would be crushed. Peter Lee had promised Terakh that the pheromones we were spreading would make the animals believe that the Proteo was a top-rank herd leader, but we had only the words of an addled megalomaniac for it. Maybe that was the reason he had drunk himself into a stupor at breakfast.

However, events proved Lee to be right. After one hour we reached the attack position without having experienced any problems.

When I glimpsed the coastal cliffs ahead, beyond a shambling hulk, I said: "Now," and shut down the pheromone fan. Linda cut the speed and let the monsters slither past us. Soon the whole herd has overtaken us, and we had unobstructed view to the sides. When the ice-buggies roared past us, I flipped another switch, launching our rockets with a loud whoosh. Peter Lee revived for a moment and shouted a slurred "Hurrah!"

A dozen rockets flew in an arc above the leviathans and struck the cliffs several hundred yards ahead of them. The well-composed scents of their smoke trails lured the monsters forward into the Russians' tents and vehicles.

A fight in a French adventure film looks dramatic and comprehensible. The heroes do exactly the right things to prevail, preferably elegantly, too, while their enemies fall for their bullets, all actions displayed in nice camera angles. In reality a battle is a matter of horror, explosions, smoke, and confusion.

The Proteo lingered in the rear while a couple of hundred intelligent beings did their best to kill one another inside and outside those cliffs. I did not bother to use the binocular, because I did not want to see the carnage close up. Occasional smoke puffs fluttered out of holes in the cliffs and we heard distant detonations. The leviathans got dispersed in the raucous chaos and fled the area – a small-calibre bullet will only nick them but that still hurts – and Linda had to move the Proteo out of harm's way at several occasions.

Linda and I crossed the battleground on foot with our faces behind protective masks and our backpacks crammed with equipment. Peter Lee remained in the Proteo. I would report to him whenever he got sober. Two ursine braves escorted us through a mess of crushed vehicles to the edge of the ice sheet and across a small rocky beach cluttered with corpses to a wide opening in the cliff face. Linda looked ahead with a stiff neck and squeezed my hand through thick mittens. I focused on taking one step at a time without stepping on a body or slipping on the ice.

Will this be our fate, too? That's the only thought that stuck in my mind during that walk. The ursines seemed unaffected, but what did I know of their mentality? Veteran soldiers have their emotions dulled by combat, though sometimes they crack under the pressure of war and turn into shivering mental cases or raging beasts. Does that happen to other intelligent species, too? Well, I leave that issue to the anthropologists.

Standing at the opening, I said: "This is an artificial cave mouth." The technical words camouflaged my fear. "Look, the walls and the ceilings are too even. I think this is or has been a mine."

I gazed up along the steep cliff side. Some openings far above us were easy to spot while other looked like patches of shadow on the granite. A Russian diesel generator chuffed next to the opening, its exhaust pipe spewing wisps of stinking smoke. Bullets had dented its metal housing. A bundle of thick cables carried electricity into the mountain.

The daylight reached some distance into the tunnel, but soon we entered chthonian darkness. Most of the light bulbs strung on cables along the ceiling had been destroyed in the fighting. Our electric torches and a chain of ursine oil lanterns attempted to dispel the dark, though with little success. Far ahead a cluster of spotlights illuminated a big bulky object. Occasional gunshots echoed in the distance. Maybe some Russians kept on fighting down in the pits or, more likely, trigger-happy ursines fired at fluttering shadows.

A restless Terakh waited for us at the spotlights about three hundred feet into the mountain. They formed a circle around an elevator. Gunshots had shattered a few, but enough were shining to provide decent illumination. Five humans in stained winter uniforms and two ursines lay dead around it. Ten yards beyond them I saw in a sturdy rack of steel rods holding a metal cylinder, six foot tall and two foot in diameter.

The tunnel continued into the mountain, a route marked with more oil lanterns. I pointed my torchlight at the cylinder: its shell had the same red shade as the strange stove in major Akhmatov's hideout. The words Мольния Царя were stencilled on its lateral surface in the same font and colour as the text on that stove.

"Linda, what does that say?" I whispered.

"I can only make out the words *mol'níya tsárya*. It means 'the tsar's thunderbolt'. But there seem to be words in small print below it."

Shit! Another sign of the Russians' advanced technology, I thought. I made an effort to keep my voice calm. "We'll check it in a moment." I turned to Terakh and made a slight bow.

66

He addressed us and Linda translated: "This facility is secured. I want you to go down with the elevator. You will find one of my braves three drifts down and he will direct you to something important."

"Certainly. I'd just like to take a look at that cylinder first," I said. *Will he sense my nervousness?*

"Why? It's just some sort of barrel," Terakh said.

"I'd like to confirm that," I said.

Terakh remained in place without speaking, so I walked around him and motioned Linda to come along. His eyes followed us, but I could not read his inhuman face.

"Does it say the same things as on the red stove? Speak quietly," I whispered.

"In parts, yes. It says: 'Hazard. The unit contains explosives. The unit contains substances that emit ionizing radiation. The unit contains toxic substances. The unit may only be handled by authorized specialists.' What do you think this is?" mumbled Linda.

"Djävlar!" The insight made me lose my composure. For the first since my arrival in Alba, I spoke in Swedish. Linda grunted something and I switched to English. "Apologies for that curse. It is an infernal device. I'll explain later."

Linda nodded.

I forced myself to remain calm while scrutinizing the cylinder. Its top could be unbolted and detached with proper tools. A mechanism was attached to its centre, a square, six by six inches, with sixteen black buttons arranged four by four. When the beam of my torchlight rested on them, I saw that each was labelled with a yellow Cyrillic letter.

"That's the sixteen initial letters in the Russian alphabet," said Linda.

"Ask Terakh if he knows who the dead Russians are?" I said.

Linda translated and I understood the answer without interpretation: "No."

Two Russians had officers' rank insignia. I checked their pockets. Most items were of little interest, but I found a piece of paper with ten block letters written by hand. They were all on that set of buttons. The note disappeared discreetly into one of my pockets.

"Have you taken any prisoners?" I asked.

"Only a few civilians. All enemy soldiers are dead. We usually don't take prisoners. It's too cumbersome to keep them alive," answered Terakh through Linda.

I shivered. *What calm cruelty.* "How did those Russians die?"

"They came up in the elevator when we stormed the entry tunnel and they were killed here in a melee." Terakh moved his feet in that restless "gesture" I had seen before. "Never mind them. Go down at once."

Linda and I entered the elevator cage, which was attached to three vertical iron bars going down in the dark. Its steel mesh railing ended just above my waist. It could carry four humans but an ursine would probably consider it unpleasantly cramped even if he used it alone. The bright roundel from Linda's electric torch moved across the control panel, neatly labelled in Russian, and she pressed a button.

The cage shook and started to descend slowly. I pointed the torchlight's beam straight down but did not see the bottom. The cage quivered when the electrical engine unrolled the elevator cable, but I felt secure because this was a sturdy construction.

"The elevator is a later installation," said Linda. "It does not match the tunnel or the shaft. Wrong proportions." Her voice was devoid of emotions.

"Is this a Russian mine?" I asked.

"I don't think so. It is too wide and too well excavated. Look at the bedrock." Her electric torch made tiny quartz crystals glitter one foot from my face. The cage descended so slowly that I could touch that rock easily. The surface was surprisingly smooth. Its dull sheen spoke of old age.

"I don't know of any machine that can drill a polished pit like this," I said.

"The dinosaurs," said Linda.

"What?!"

"Don't take me literally. But this mine seems to be older than mankind's arrival in Alba. The ursines must have had a golden age a long time ago," said Linda.

"God alone know," I said. "Regardless what the Russians have found, they've kept it well hidden. The Institute knows nothing of this."

"If the ursines once upon a time drilled this pit, they must have been very advanced," said Linda.

"The entry tunnel looks less sophisticated. The mine must have been excavated in two phases. That'd explain why the miners' technology improved," I said. "And recently the Russians put this elevator here."

"What was that infernal bomb we saw up there?" asked Linda.

"I think the Russians have made a transuranium bomb. The physicist Leo Szilard claims that such a device would be equal to thousands of ordinary bombs." In my mind I wished for his presence. *He would know what to do with it.*

"Why would the Russians put that weapon here?" said Linda.

"They really want to keep this place out of their enemies' hands. We were incredibly lucky that those officers were killed before they could activate it," I said.

Linda and I breathed heavily as we struggled to cross a long stretch of rubble in the partially ruined tunnel. Our bulky polar clothes and heavy backpacks hampered all movements. No ursine would have been able to penetrate this deep into the mine, because that had required climbing ladders.

The wound in my chest ached every time I used my hands for support and whenever the mittens touched stone, cold jabbed at my fingers. The beam of my torchlight searched in front of us for something that was not rock. A brief gleaming attracted my attention. "There is something metallic maybe thirty yards ahead," I called.

Linda let her light beam probe in that direction.

Spindly, glittering – what is it? We put our backpacks on the ground and advanced. Worry burned in my belly. Nothing living should be down here, but what you don't know is always a potential threat.

Suddenly I was able to puzzle together the disparate impressions that my eyes had perceived in the darkness. "Dinosaurs or Martians … you were right!"

"Bože moi!" whispered Linda.

A metal spider, fifteen yards across – no, it's a machine, a vehicle, I thought. *This hasn't been constructed in Prague or Paris, not in Magalhana, Africa or Alba.*

The thing's design was utterly alien – unknown creatures had long ago built a walking mining vehicle. Now it rested here, stiff and decayed, coped up behind long stretches of rubble. We also glimpsed scientific tools that its Russian discoverers had abandoned a few hours ago as they dashed away to man the barricades: ordinary cameras, notebooks, and pencils.

"What are we supposed to do?" My voice echoed in the dark.

"Look up there, the controls." Linda's torchlight guided me to the right spot on the machine's back. "Help me up."

I clasped my hands for her foot and hoisted her upward so that she reached the control nest. She slid into a place too cramped for a human operator.

Meanwhile, I scanned the ground with my electric torch. A few papers here and there, all in Russian. A sheet with Cyrillic letters in longhand next to aliens characters. I put them in my backpack.

Beyond the machine I reached a rough rock face: the end of the tunnel. It was pockmarked where drills had penetrated it, but those hollows had a dull texture. Millennia had oxidized the naked surfaces. A drill bit was still stuck in the stone. The machine must have broken down and been abandoned.

Food and hot beverage are essential in severe cold. Linda and I shared a bowl of meat soup cooked on our camping stove while we recapitulated what we had discovered.

"The driver was no more than five foot tall, but he must've had very long arms," said Linda and made an estimate between her outstretched hands.

I could not imagine what the machine's designers had looked like. "Hmm, that's like a big gibbon. But are you sure that the operator had only two arms?"

"No, I'm not," said Linda. "Something else. The metal pieces have fused together. Nothing can be moved. That's a process that would take a lot of time. I think this machine has been here for more than a hundred thousand years."

It was certainly advantageous to let a skilled mechanic investigate such matters. "There were no civilizations on Earth in those times… claim those archaeologists that have been digging all over the world for more than a century."

"Rubbish… so it seems." Linda, too, sounded overawed by the discovery.

"What the hell do we tell Lee?" I dithered between lying and speaking the truth.

Linda did not hesitate: "The truth. Someone else will tell him sooner or later."

"The obvious facts, yes. But we should keep our conclusions and hypotheses to ourselves. Let him figure that out by himself. Our faked 'ignorance' might serve as a card up the sleeve," I said.

Linda interrupted me: "Listen here. Russians don't commit suicide. They probably planned to disassemble and remove that spider machine and then blow the mine to smithereens."

She is right; the Japanese kill themselves for their emperor, but not the Russians, I thought. "Skilful of them to keep this matter secret for so long. That indicates that they only have uncovered a few other archaeological artefacts." I switched subject. "I have found a piece of paper that may contain the bomb's activation code."

Linda nodded and emptied her mug. "We've got to return to the Proteo before we get too exhausted from the cold."

We slept for hours in the warm Proteo to regain our strength. When I woke, I had had enough of Alba. No more icy plains, no more cold air grating in my lungs. When will I rest on a sunny beach where children play in the waves?

Linda's hand touched my scalp. "I've cooked some food. Mr Lee is awake, too."

Lee held a cup of coffee in his hand. "Good morning Mr Bornewald. Now I'd like to know what's hidden inside that mountain." The voice was clearer and the eyes sharper, but the face remained stiff. The pain in his leg had not subsided, I concluded.

No beating around the bush, I thought, "A big red metal cylinder labelled 'the tsar's thunderbolt' in Russian and a huge mining machine of indeterminate age, manufactured by an unknown civilization."

Lee was quiet for some time before responding with a question: "Concerning that last claim, are you sure?"

"Both of us are." I stressed the word both, because Lee's habit of addressing me as if Linda was not present irritated me.

"Can we get that machine out of the mine?" he asked.

"No. Too much rubble in the way," I said.

"Who ...?" he said.

"No idea," I said.

"How old?" he said.

"The passage of time has fused its metal parts together," I said.

He grunted and sipped some coffee. "An eon ... that was the old Greeks' word for a god's life span."

May God help me, I thought. *How do I manoeuvre in this minefield?*

"That red cylinder ... what can you tell me about it?" Lee asked.

Linda's quick response made him turns his eyes in her direction: "It's labelled 'Hazard. The unit contains explosives. The unit contains substances that emit ionizing radiation. The unit contains toxic substances. The unit may only be handled by authorized specialists.'"

As soon as she stopped talking, Lee's gaze returned to me. "What does that indicate?"

"Your guess is as good as mine." His calm rudeness annoyed me, but I forced my voice to be level, because I knew what was at stake. "I don't know."

Lee voice rose. "Hah, now we'll be able to kick the tyrants in the ..." He stopped before a foul word crossed his lips. "That's a Russian transuranium bomb." He knew surprisingly much, but his employer surely had good sources. Lee emptied the cup in one gulp. "To use a Norse metaphor: we will make Surtr dance in Alba. The despots will face their worst defeat ever."

Linda looked at me.

"Surtr is a fire demon in Scandinavian pagan legends," I said.

"That's right," said Lee. "Hephaestus Mons will spew death and destruction over the tyrants' holdings in Acheron. The transuranium bomb will blast that slumbering volcano into life."

Unleashing Götterdämmerung – insanity! I thought. "How?" The underlying question was rather: How do we stop his mad scheme? I also realized that he would kill Linda and me at once when he was done. No witnesses to reveal his titanic crime.

"We'll drop the bomb into its crater," said Lee.

"So you'll pick a large aeroplane out of the hat, just like that? And it will fly there without getting shot down by the Danes?" I asked.

"Yes, just like that. Don't underestimate me. Do you know how important Alban resources are for Russia and the Empire in the war?" he said.

Linda glanced back and forth between Lee and me. I nodded to indicate that I listened.

He continued: "There are no republican military forces here, just us spies who work with ursines that hate Russia. If we knock out most of the tyrants' operations in Alba, we will strike a mighty blow for the ursines' cause and at same time improve the republics' prospects in Europe."

His hate has no limits, I thought. "Mr Lee, I do not underestimate you." My statement addressed his madness, but he would interpret it in another way.

"Good," said Peter Lee. "Miss Connor, go and fetch Rlishi. We have to load the bomb in the Proteo at once and return to base. No time to waste."

CHAPTER 13

"Johnny, wake up."

I opened my eyes in the darkness of our room in the ursine base. Pain and nausea: once again a Maxidin hangover. I had no idea what time it was, because I had collapsed in the bed as soon as we had returned here with the Russian bomb in the Proteo.

Linda whispered in my right ear: "I had a nightmare. They killed us. We have to get out of here before they dispatch that bomb."

"If they suspect we're up to something, they'll kill us straight away," I said.

"How can we survive?" she said.

"Peter Lee is doing the same mistake all the time," I said.

"You mean that he treats me all the time like I'm stupid." Linda voice got sharper.

"Yes, that. And he looks down on me because of my skin colour. He thinks people like you and I can't be bright, brave and persistent. Also, he underestimates us because we don't carry guns. He thinks that his problems can be blown to pieces. And he is all wrong." Composing that statement in my miserable condition took time and I stuttered at several words.

"So that's why you're not carrying a gun?" said Linda.

"No, that's rather because an armed person is liable to get shot at by other armed people. If one looks harmless, it'll be easier to solve problems with guile. Anyhow, Lee doesn't realize how capable you and I are and we'll turn that against him. For instance, he doesn't know that I am a competent pilot," I said.

"Why haven't you told me that?" Linda sounded annoyed.

73

"Because it hasn't been important before. Anyhow, back home young aristocrats are expected to know how to fly. I got my first license when I was sixteen."

"Good. We should hijack Lee's aircraft and escape," said Linda.

"I agree. But we'll probably have to kill both Lee and the crew. And then we'll need to find a safe landing spot down in Acheron. We can't touch down with a stolen plane at any airfield. But we ought to be able to handle that if I only get hold of a colleague. Are you ready to kill several people in cold blood?" I tried to sound calm and confident. Should we really discuss murder like they were a simple business proposal? I had no answer to that question.

"Yes, I am. They plan to destroy my home! What about you?" Linda asked.

"I have few qualms right now." That was a lie. I did not want to kill again. "We kill to save the lives of innocent people. So be it, but let us never think that the ends would justify the means that easily."

"Ave Maria, gratia plena, Dominus tecum, benedicta tu in mulieribus et benedictus fructus ventris tui Iesus. Ave Maria, Mater Dei, ora pro nobis peccatoribus, nunc et in hora mortis nostrae. Ave Maria," Linda prayed and crossed herself.

I whispered a response: "Grant us courage and strength to block this foul plan. Amen."

"Amen," she said.

"You must find out at once how to detonate that bomb in a controlled manner." Peter Lee was too weak to sit so he addressed that order at the rock ceiling.

"Of course," I said. "Linda is on her way to the workshop to inspect the bomb."

"Make sure she doesn't foul anything up."

"Certainly," I said.

"When you two are done, I'll make sure we have an airplane. I've got contacts, I know how." Lee moaned with pain and tears filled his eyes.

Without further comments I left his room.

"Booby traps – that's what worries me right now," Linda said when she and I squatted next to the contraption of steel rods that held the red cylinder.

The workshop encompassed a wide area with benches and machine tools placed well apart to accommodate the ursines' need for space. Half a dozen mechanics were busy with vehicles and machines. Occasionally they looked in our direction, but with little curiosity. They had no idea what the

74

cylinder contained and they had probably been ordered to leave us alone. Maybe Peter Lee had not even told Rlishi.

Linda continued: "If I had designed this device, I would have installed a booby trap that is activated when someone tries to disassemble it after it has been armed. But the trap would be inactive before arming to make it possible to carry out maintenance. After all, there must be batteries inside for an ignition device and those need to be replaced or recharged every once in a while."

"That sounds reasonable. Do you want to remove the top of the cylinder straight away?" I asked.

"No way. I don't dare to assume that the Russian have reasoned like that. I need to peek inside the bomb before I open it. I am going to drill holes in the shell here, here and here." A finger touched the flat top once and the curved cylinder surface twice. "I have tapped all over it and those spots seem to have nothing underneath. Then I will insert small lamps and use a thin periscope to inspect the innards."

"Have you found a periscope here?" I asked.

"No, I'll have to make one from scratch. What do you know of metalworking?" said Linda.

"Not much," I said.

Linda looked into my eyes. "Well, I'll make you an apprentice. Follow my instructions to the letter. Or you'll kill us all."

"Yes, sir!"

We spent one day making the periscope. To me it ought to be an easy task, because that instrument is based on simple principles. But Linda had exacting standards and knew what performance she wanted. She had to be able to rotate its front mirror, which would explore the interior of the cylinder, in several directions. And when you start with a long copper tube, a piece of glass mirror and lots of nuts, bolts and metal wire, you must work long hours to reach the goal.

On the second day, we assembled the devices that would illuminate the interior: electrical lamps attached to long metal rods that I would manipulate according to Linda's instructions. That was an easier task and required only a few hours.

After lunch that day, Linda used a drill to open three holes in the cylinder casing.

"Insert the right lamp slowly and fix it. Then you do the same with the left one." Linda issued orders in a flat voice while she inserted the periscope in the hole in the cylinder top. She had to lean forward in an uncomfortable posture, but she was the one who had selected the location of that hole.

She turned the periscope cautiously and manipulated its front mirror with a small lever. "Ah, now I see." She moved the tube inward another four inches and wiggled it. "Good craftsmanship. Clever solution."

After manoeuvring the telescope for ten minutes, she retracted it and sat down. Sweat covered her forehead. I rubbed her shoulders to alleviate the tension while I waited for her assessment of the situation.

"I need another session before I am content," she said.

This time she worked for more than twenty minutes and ordered me to move the lamps this way and that. Suddenly she extracted the periscope and leaned at the bomb rack. "The keyboard on the top lid is an electromechanical device. If the keys are pressed in the right order, a switch will be flipped, which activates a timer. There is a booby trap. If someone removes the lid after the activation of the timer, the bomb will detonate immediately."

"Well done, sir." I softly punched my fist at her left shoulder as a boyish salute. She smiled back.

"Let's steel ourselves for the next step. Do you want to tell Peter Lee that you have the activation code?" she asked.

"It'd be better if you come up with a way of bypassing the keyboard. Then we can keep the code as an ace up the sleeve," I said.

Linda nodded. "I'll have to remove the lid first and inspect the timer. We must figure out how you set it. That step will take till tomorrow. I'm also going to seal the new holes to keep out dirt."

"Good. When you're done, I'll have a talk with Lee and we'll find out what he wants," I said.

We proceeded during the afternoon by making a stand of steel rods. It was to be placed next to the bomb. Linda planned to detach the lid and carefully shift it to the stand. We would then pull it away from bomb about one and a half foot. That would enable us to keep all cables in place without stretching them too much. Then Linda would inspect the interior of cylinder.

When we executed the plan the next day, we encountered no problems and when evening came, we were able to reattach the lid. The Russians had installed robust easy-to-use mechanisms in the bomb's innards, so there was little risk for mishaps. Linda also understood how to set the timer and how to hotwire the keyboard. She had disconnected it and experimented with letter sequence I had found on the dead officer: it was the correct one, just as I had assumed. The bomb was ready for use – now we had to get ready for our escape.

"Mr Lee, we've completed the job." I looked at an addled and dirty Peter Lee, who huddled on his bed. He shook the head slightly and focused his eyes on my face. The air stank of liquor and illness.

Linda remained in our room, exhausted after the demanding hours in the workshop. She did not want to face Peter Lee tonight. I would also have preferred to abstain, but somebody had to do it.

"Well done, B'rnwald. I'll reques' that airpl'n," he slurred. "If things g'm'way, we'll drop th' bom' in two days. Th' gates of hell'll open for the' tyran's."

Raving mad, I thought. "We'll need a cargo parachute, too. The bomb must land safely inside the crater. If it smashes into the ground, it won't work."

"I see. I'll take care of that."

Linda and I waited with covered faces and protective goggles at the entrance to the large cavern. An icy wind swept along the cliff face and pummelled us, but our polar clothes ensured that we would endure its attention. The sun, high in the sky, made the ice glitter all the way to the horizon. Three ursines stood next to us, seemingly unaffected by the cold. The bomb rested in its rack on a sled behind us, next to a simple movable crane built by the ursines. They had also dragged some barrels of aviation fuel and a hand pump from a dump.

The bomb was not red any longer. Yesterday, while Linda and I waited for Peter Lee to confirm that the transport plane would arrive as requested, we had used the available time to paint it medium grey to make it less conspicuous.

Aeroplane engines buzzed in the distance, the noise increasing for every second.

"How come Lee and the ursines possess all these resources?" I whispered to Linda. That question had churned in my mind for many days.

"Well, if a European government stands behind them it'd be possible." Linda kept her voice low, to, but seemed unconcerned.

"It isn't that easy. This ursine base – no republic is able to sponsor it from the other side of the world. Also, the fighting in Europe devours all resources that the republics possess," I said.

"Maybe the Orange State is involved?" said Linda.

"That's one possibility. They have the gold to pay for it." I still felt doubtful. "Unsavoury co-belligerents, anyhow."

"These ursines belong to a powerful clan federation as far as I have learned by listening. But I've no idea who their leaders are. There are lots of ursines that hate humans in general and Russians in particular," said Linda.

"And we'll let those aliens play in our team?" My question was rhetorical.

"When in dire straits…" mumbled Linda.

"I don't want our cause to be corrupted." I was not ready to budge on that issue.

"Lee seems less determined than you in that regard," said Linda.

I nodded. "Are you ready?"

"As ready as one can get." Linda voice had lost that confident edge. She suddenly squeezed my hand through the thick mittens.

What sane person will ever feel ready to kill? I thought.

The aeroplane approached from the north. I raised my binocular and zoomed in a carmine twin-engine biplane. The landing gears were equipped with both wheels and skis. The name of the owner was painted in white along the fuselage: *Boelcke Luftfahrt AG.*

"A Blériot 230N bush plane," I said. "Decent cargo capacity and a good range."

The plane flew over us at a low altitude, turned into the wind and descended to the ice. The pilot parried a few gusts of wind and put her down smoothly. That fellow knew his line of work. I wouldn't be able to fly that well, because so far I had only piloted smaller planes. The Blériot taxied up to the cavern entrance, turned the tail in our direction and came to a halt twenty yards away.

Two men climbed out of the cockpit when the engines had stopped. They were covered by bulky electro-heated overalls and lumbered toward us. My back stiffened by sudden pain: these two unknown men would soon be killed by us.

"Guten Tag. I am captain Boelcke," said one of them in the dialect of Saxony. "This is pilot Arnold. You two, are you my mechanics?"

"Jawohl, Herr Kapitän," I said quickly to hide my annoyance with his haughty manner.

He pointed at the bomb. "Make sure that that thing is secure fastened in the cargo hold. Use a weld if you need. Make sure that your assistant tops the tanks. I will inspect everything before take-off. Arnold will come out every thirty minutes and run the engines to keep them warm." His phrasing showed that he believed that Linda was a boy; unsurprising, because the arctic clothes camouflaged her gender.

"Of course," I said.

Boelcke and Arnold continued into the cavern, while Linda and I hurried over the ice to the Blériot. The ursines pulled the crane behind us. Linda opened the cargo door on the starboard side of the fuselage and started to inspect the deck to decide how she would secure the bomb rack to it. I sneaked into the cockpit to check one important function. The instrumentation was familiar and I found what I was looking for: two buttons for electrical starters. The pilot could kick-start the engines from his seat without outside help, a practical arrangement in polar lands. My knees wobbled for an instant from relief and then I returned to the cargo hold with light steps.

"We won't have to kill," I whispered in Linda's ear while she crawled over the deck to check the eyelets.

"Dei gratia," she said and I saw how her tense body relaxed. "Thanks Johnny."

Two hours of hard work ensued, during which pilot Arnold came out every half hour to run the engines for a while, but he generally ignored us. That attitude suited us perfectly.

When everything was ready, Linda sent the ursines to fetch the pilots. While they were away, we entered the cockpit, and got into the pilots' seats. I pressed the ignition buttons and the engines started with no hassle. I hardly believed my eyes when we accelerated into the wind and left the base behind us. The scheme had succeeded far better than I had ever hoped, and that just because Lee and Boelcke consistently had misjudged Linda and me.

I pulled the wheel toward me and the Blériot slowly ascended into the dark blue sky. Some cloud tufts provided the only contrast. *Freedom, freedom. They can't keep us shackled no more*, I triumphed in my mind. The plane trembled under my inexperienced hands, but it obeyed every command. Soon I lowered its nose to level flight. Now it was time to fix our position and set the course to Acheron.

CHAPTER 14

"Linda, you must take the controls now." The propeller din forced me to shout. We had been flying for half an hour toward Hephaestus Mons, an uneven snow-capped cone at the horizon. Fredriksborg lay somewhere behind it, but we could not go there with a stolen aircraft. The Blériot cruised at 120 knots and the weather favoured us for the moment: sunshine and a steady wind from behind. "I need to use the radio to reach a colleague. It'll be easy to keep the plane on course."

After a moment's hesitation, Linda gripped the co-pilot's controls. I explained how to handle the wheel and the pedals. Her stressful breathing produced white wisps in the cold air. After ten minutes I said: "Now you know enough. Keep everything steady and you'll do fine."

Linda nodded.

I moved to the signalman's nook behind the cockpit, where an Uher Beta, a sturdy radio made in Brünn, waited for me. While warming its tubes, I prepared my message in German, encrypted parts of it and translated the individual letters to the dashes and dots of the signal alphabet. When the apparatus was ready, I started to tap a call at 137 myriacycles per second: "S-C-H-W-A-R-Z-E-R F-U-C-H-S S-U-C-H-T F-I-G-A-R-O". The cold hurt my exposed hand.

Two or three minutes later I perceived a response in the buzzing earphones. I jotted down its dashes and dots: "Figaro here, Figaro here. Go to the well for water. Over." That was the correct identification phrase.

I confirmed: "A wedding requires green wine. Over."

"Understood. Begin. Over."

I tapped a series of seemingly random letters and digits, my brief encrypted message.

"L-I-L-A F-U-E-N-F." Those words confirmed that the message had arrived and that a response would come within three minutes. I put my hand in the mitten and sighed with relief. "Linda, how are doing?"

"Quite well," she said.

"Five to eight minutes, then I'll take over the controls again," I said.

The earphones started to tap three minutes later and I jotted down every dot and dash. I deciphered the text with hands that got clumsier and clumsier from the cold. A glance at a map of the Sea of Tears transformed its latitude and longitude to a geographical location. We would reach that spot in a few hours, though with little fuel remaining in the tanks.

"Now I am done. I just have to thaw my hands before I take the controls." I got into the pilot's seat. The fingers ached while getting warmed by the electrical pilot gloves. "Do you know the Rasmussen Bay in the Sea of Tears?"

"I know where it is on a map, but no more," Linda said.

"We're going there to meet one of my colleagues. I'll take the controls now." A moment later, I put the plane in a shallow starboard turn to a new course.

When we reached Acheron, patches of brown and black vegetation appeared in the white landscape and they grew wider the further downslope we got. I put the plane in a shallow dive to stay at two thousand feet above ground. Here and there cattle grazed on the slopes and soon we spotted the first tilled fields bordered by dry-stone fences. The temperature increased, a relief for our weary bodies. Far ahead I glimpsed the Sea of Tears, or at least so I imagined.

"Give me a Maxidin pill. I'm getting sluggish." I spoke with reluctance. I wanted to quit that drug for good, but now I had to complete this flight without food and rest.

Linda got a pill from my medikit, pushed aside my face mask and put it in my mouth. I swallowed and in a minute or two the drug swept like a fresh spring breeze through my body and banished the feeling of exhaustion. I smiled, even though I knew this was phony joy.

Three hours and 400 miles later we cruised 11,000 feet below the ice sheet along a narrow deep river that was labelled *Grieg-fluß* on the map. The air was warm compared to what we had endured during the past few weeks. The barometer touched 45 inches mercury, one and a half times the atmospheric pressure at the ice sheet, so breathing was easy. The sky had changed to a paler blue.

The Rasmussen fiord jabbed like a dagger into the mainland eleven miles ahead and its tip served as the Grieg River estuary. Steep hills surrounded it, bare grey rock mixed with meadows covered by black grass and shrubberies. I spotted scattered ursine settlements with the characteristic wide circular huts, but no signs of human presence. That was advantageous, because the news of our arrival would spread more slowly among settlers without radios. In minutes, I would cross the estuary at 1,000 feet and the agreed meeting spot was less than five minutes away down the fiord.

"Where will we land?" said Linda.

"That'll be tricky. I need three thousand feet of flat open ground for a safe touchdown. There aren't any such spaces in sight," I said. The fuel indicator showed that we could fly for another forty minutes so I felt no urgency.

When the Blériot crossed the shoreline, I descended to 600 feet. Far ahead I glimpsed a streak of black smoke rising from the water. *A sea-borne reception committee?* I thought. The seconds ticked by. The afternoon sun gleamed in west beyond the black landscape. *Yes, that's a ship!*

A small blocky vessel with a single smokestack producing a pillar of coal smoke steamed in our direction at the agreed-upon position. I circled above her and waited for a signal. At her stern I saw a red flag with a white, green, and red canton, the flag of New England. Three signal rockets rose from the foredeck: blue, white, and green – the colours of the Nobel Institute. We had arrived at the right place. Only touchdown remained.

"Is this the reception you expected?" said Linda.

"No, not the ship," I said. *Has Figaro assumed that we have a floatplane?*

"Who are on that ship?" Linda asked.

"I only know my colleague Figaro. The others are unknown," I said.

I turned the plane and continued along the fiord in search for a decent landing spot, but without success. "It'll be an emergency touchdown." My voice stuttered from tension. "I'll go down on a lakeside meadow, facing the water because of the wind. It'll be shaky. We'll end up in the water so fetch life jackets, please."

Linda returned presently and strapped life jackets on us.

"Right above your head, you see a hatch in the ceiling. You must open it to give us an escape route if the plane starts sinking.

Linda looked straight up and nodded. "I understand."

I continued: "Good. Get up and stand on the seat. Hold on to some steady with one hand and unlatch the hatch with the other. Then get down and get belted. Repeat what I said."

Linda repeated exactly what I had said.

"Good. Get moving," I said.

The hatch slid down and rearward. A roaring whirlwind swept through the cockpit, tossing about papers and loose objects. Conversation was no longer possible, but it did not matter – we were ready.

I turned the Blériot toward the meadow I had selected. We made a wide circle while I nudged the plane down to 40 feet above ground and reduced its speed. Earlier I had only piloted single-engine planes and now I would crash-land a much heavier craft. My handed trembled when the Blériot reached the edge of the meadow.

I shut off both engines. The wheels hit ground. The fuselage quaked and the landing gears groaned. Linda and I bounced in the seats. I struggled to keep a straight course. The starboard landing gear buckled with a gunshot sound after 150 yards. A wing struck the ground and snapped. The starboard engine was torn loose and disappeared to the rear. The plane slewed violently to the right and the twist fractured the port landing gear. The fuselage struck the ground with a thud that pushed the air out of my lungs. The plane skidded sideways across the black grass. The fuselage hit the water, white foam sprayed in all directions and we stopped with a jolt.

I took a deep breath, uncoupled the safety belt and leaned over to Linda. She was shaken but conscious. I opened her safety belt and urged her upward. She moved through the open hatch and I followed her into safety on top of the fuselage with my backpack in a firm grip.

We had been lucky. The Blériot rested in a stable position ten yards from the beach. The top of the fuselage was several inches above the waves, but I heard the gurgling of water seeping into the aircraft. The plane was wreck, but it had not caught fire.

Linda huddled close to me, gripped my arm and mumbled: "Johnny, Johnny, you made it."

I could not answer because of battle jitters: my vocal chords did not obey my will. A salt-smelling breeze caressed my face. Low waves lapped the fuselage. All was well – we had survived the ice inferno and that felt like crawling out of a dark cramped cave into sunlight. The ship approached us slowly. Now we merely had to wait for our rescuers to pick us up and provide hot food and soft bunks.

The ship stopped more than a hundred yards away and launched a dinghy manned by two sailors. Both were young and wore blue trousers, black knitted sweaters and navy blue knitted caps. The tallest of them hailed us in German: *"Ohoi, schwarzer Fuchs!"* His accent indicated that it was not his native language.

"That's me," I responded in the same language, "but where is Figaro? I know him."

"Aboard the *Nereid*. We'll take you there," he called.

"We've got the jitters so come and help us."

They approached the fuselage. The short rower grabbed a wing strut and held the dinghy in place while the other one helped us aboard. His face, adorned with thick glasses, looked familiar, but I could not place it. He scrutinized me, as if he had a similar experience. The dinghy shifted restlessly when I planted my feet on the deck, a pleasantly familiar feeling. I stretched out at the bow, faced the sky and listened at the gurgling of the prow cutting through the water. It felt almost like my youthful excursions in the Kattegat; only the screeching seagulls were missing.

A seaman on the *Nereid* lowered a rope ladder and he and the rowers assisted Linda and me. The ship had a low freeboard, because the Sea of Tears is a lake, not an ocean, but those yards were still hard to climb. Her captain waited for us, a man I knew well: Paul von Rosen, my old schoolmate and the institute agent called Figaro. He was two inches shorter than me, swarthy with a wispy beard, a peaked cap, a leather jacket and navy blue pants. I let him initiate the conversation.

"I'm Sebastian Thorn, master of the *Nereid*," he said in English. In our line of business, you change name as often as you buy new shirts. "Welcome aboard, Miss...?" He extended his hand to Linda.

She shook it. "Miss Linda Connor."

He turned to me and waited for my greeting.

"Good day, captain Thorn," I said in English, shook his hand and entered the role-playing game in the customary manner. "I'm Johnny Bornewald from the Netherlands."

"Welcome, sir. I am happy we could rescue you."

"Thanks a lot, captain," I said

"I have ordered the cook to prepare something hot. Please come to my cabin and he'll serve it there." Paul gestured towards an open hatch.

The meat stew was filling and spicy, just the right thing after our hardships. Linda and I occupied a narrow couch while Paul had unfolded a wooden stool in front of us. The cabin was cramped, but no worse than inside a cloudship. I felt at ease.

"You – a skipper under New England's flag," I said.

"Well, I never thought I'd catch you falling out of the sky in Alba," said Paul.

Time is short. No beating around the bush, I thought. "One major matter must be taken care. There is a barrel inside the wreck. We must salvage it."

"Can't be done. The plane is in shallow water and the *Nereid* cannot get close enough to use the deck crane," said Paul.

"It's a transuranium bomb," I said in a low voice.

Paul turned and gazed at the Blériot through an open porthole.

"I've a suggestion, provided that you have an acetylene torch," said Linda.

"I'm listening," said Paul.

"I can open a big hole in the roof of the fuselage and detach the bomb from its rack. We attach a long chain to the bomb and the ship's crane. The *Nereid* tows the plane to deeper water and we hoist the bomb to the deck. I need two assistants," said Linda.

"How confident are you that this scheme will work?" asked Paul.

"I am an experienced mechanic. I secured the bomb in that cargo bay. It did not break lose at the crash. Bloody hell, I know what to do." Exhaustion cracked Linda's temper.

Paul looked at me.

"Trust her," I said. "She has never disappointed me."

"Well, Miss Connor, are you up to doing all that after the meal? I'd love to get out of here quickly."

Linda nodded. "I'm tired, but not too tired."

"Johnny, you look wasted," said Paul.

"Yeah, Maxidin has kept me going for too many hours. I'm getting addicted," I said.

"That stuff is a treacherous ally. I quit using it years ago," said Paul. "Anyhow, the steward is busy preparing a cabin for you. Two bunks in a shoebox."

"That'll do fine," I said.

Linda nodded in agreement.

CHAPTER 15

I woke in the lower bunk still wearing all my clothes. Four heartbeats followed before I understood where I was. The rhythmic pulse from the *Nereid's* engine indicated that we were on the way somewhere, so the salvage operations must have been completed. A short swell rocked the ship gently. I checked my watch: early evening, darkness outside the porthole and time for a meal. A Maxidin hangover wracked my body, but I forced myself to ignore it.

My nose guided me through the *Nereid's* innards to the mess, where Linda and three sailors were sharing a meal. They were the pair that had picked us up at the aeroplane wreck and a weather-beaten thin man in his thirties. I was still unable to remember where I had seen that familiar face before. The quartet mixed English and Russian. The tone of the conversation and the Linda's body language showed that the men saw her as their equal. She must have done well during the salvage operation.

I fetched a bowl of fish and potatoes from the cook and joined the quartet.

"Hello, I'm Yitzchak Asimoff." The familiar sailor spoke with a Russian accent. He took a close look at me through thick lenses that made his eyes look small. I guessed he was a few years younger than me.

"Johnny Bornewald." I said.

"Robert Kagan," said the other rower. His native language must be Russian, too.

"Tom Dinn," said the third man, an Englishman judging from his dialect. He wore a green overall and was weather-beaten in that pale manner that I had seen among so many people living in Acheron where the sunlight was weak.

86

The food was filling and I was too hungry to care much about its lack of flavour. My headache diminished as soon as the belly got filled.

Yitzchak looked at me again and said: "S/S *Pearl*, Blekinge to Friesland. You were an ordinary seaman."

"Yes, I remember that voyage." Now the pieces fell into place. "My elder brother was responsible for that operation." Everything had worked out fine: no coast guard cutters, no torpedo boats, and no navy seaplanes.

"We were more than a hundred refugees. Why would you remember a frightened boy when you had the hands full with saving us?" said Yitzchak.

"That was a tough night, wasn't it? Quite hard wind," I said.

"I puked till I thought I would die. Anyhow, thank you. We got a new start – new lives," he said.

"I am happy to hear that." A cliché, yes, but I meant it.

"These chaps and I have salvaged the barrel," said Linda.

"The plane has disappeared in deep water," added Robert.

"Good. Bloody good," I said. *What will we do now with that monster bomb?* I was still too weary to come up with any good ideas. "Any news from the war?"

"The clashes on the southern ice plain continue, according to the radio broadcasts. The Russians have suffered setbacks," said Robert. "The Japan-Juliusburg alliance is making progress. The Danes worry about an attack on Christianshus, because if the Japanese want to crush the Russian strongpoints in Acheron, their best good route passes through Danish territory. And in the northern hemisphere the Japanese have defeated the Russian Pacific Fleet near Port Arthur."

"Two appalling allies for the rebellion," said Yitzchak.

"You fellows are as republican as I am, aren't you?" I said.

"Certainly," said Robert.

"Why do you man a New Englander ship? The Boston Puritans dislike Jews, don't they?" The *Nereid's* flag had been a riddle to me ever since I sighted here in the Rasmussen Fiord.

"The captain fixed it and he might want to tell you his version of the tale. By the way, Tom is the only able seaman around the table," said Robert.

"These chaps are my snobbish apprentices," said Tom in a jovial manner. "I do my best to keep them from drowning."

"We've survived so far," said Yitzchak. "Robert and I are scholars from Leiden University. I'm a graduate student in biochemistry and Robert in zoology. Our professors want us to do some research here in Alba."

"Are you willing to explain that?" I asked.

"Well, we're in the same boat in several ways and it is not classified information. Have you heard of 'macrobiological warfare'?" said Robert.

"No," I said.

"The use of the existing local flora and fauna for military purposes. We suspect that one or more parties are experimenting with that is Alba," said Robert.

"I've seen that. Have you heard of a zoologist called Peter Lee?" I said.

Robert and Yitzchak nodded, while Tom shook his head.

I continued: "Linda and I used the crashed Blériot to escape from his clutches. He demonstrated how to use leviathans as living tanks."

Robert exclaimed something in Russian, got a strained look on his face and glanced at Linda. But she ignored his words.

"Doctor Lee is a biochemist from Cambridge University. A skilled scientist and a devoted republican. He got into some snarl with the English security police in 1938 and vanished out of sight," said Yitzchak.

"He used pheromones to control a herd of leviathans." I summarized the battle for Post 14 in a few sentences.

"Great," said Yitzchak. "That's solid proof. So far we've only found circumstantial evidence. Can you give us a more detailed description?"

"Tomorrow," said Linda. "I must hit the sack."

I had emptied my bowl and felt less miserable, but I was still exhausted. "I agree. Tomorrow, gentlemen."

CHAPTER 16

"Did you sleep well?" said Paul von Rosen in Swedish while pouring me a cup of weak coffee.

Paul had summoned me for a breakfast in his cabin, while Linda ate with Robert and Yitzchak in the mess. Porridge bowls, sandwiches and cups crowded his desk next to nautical charts and maritime handbooks. A radio set, a big piece of elegant carpentry bolted to a bulkhead, provided operetta music from Radio Austria Intercontinental.

I looked out through the stern portholes at the sea and the sky, the elements of my heart. The light of the rising sun glittered in the short waves. "The first peaceful night since Fredriksborg." It was a pleasure to speak my native tongue again. I emptied my cup before continuing: "Your ship, she surprised me. I'm not up to date about the Institute's activities, but I never imagined that she would have a ship down here."

"It's a sordid story," said Paul. "Officially this is an oceanology research vessel financed by the New England colony. In reality, the Institute runs the show. The New England consul on Neue Trieste had gotten into a mess. Puritans abroad often go astray among worldly temptations. He took the wrong kind of person to his bed and got blackmailed. If the authorities in Boston had heard the slightest whiff, the consul would be behind bars for 'crimes against nature'. Someone told me and I proposed a solution. The consul accepted it and has become a trusted partner, at least as long as I am around to keep him on his toes."

"A solution?" I asked.

"Well, Neue Trieste is a rough place. I hired a few heavies and they had a talk with the blackmailers. The consul sweetened the proposal with some gold and suddenly everyone agreed that nothing untoward had happened."

89

"The war wrecks our souls," I said. Before the rebellion, I could not have imagined that Paul or I would tarnish our aristocratic honour with blackmail and murder; nor would the Institute have condoned such actions. *When had the rules changed? By whom? By us?*

"Yes, that's what war does to you," said Paul. "Time is always short, so you do what is necessary to go on without delays. The future is at stake. So our scruples wither away day by day."

"Point taken. When Linda and I planned our escape in the Blériot, we intended to murder three men in cold blood. They were only saved by their own misjudgements," I said.

"Enough philosophizing," said Paul. "Tell me what you've done here in Alba."

I spent ten minutes explaining what had happened between the *Cassiopeia's* arrival in Fredriksborg and our landing at the Rasmussen Fiord.

"Great job. Miss Connor is amazing. You'd be dead without her," said Paul.

"I know." I contemplated the present for a few seconds before saying. "What's the next step? What's your task here?"

Paul responded with a question: "Do you think Lee will survive?"

"That would require hospital care, but I don't know whether his allies are willing or able to provide that. Without it, he'll die within a few days," I said.

Paul nodded. "What are your plans for the barrel?"

"I want to take it to the institute. The Z boffins need to take a look at it," I said.

"We can go to any port along the Sea of Tears and you can take the barrel overland from there to Fredriksborg. And then Leclerc will have to fly it to Magalhana. And then on to Europe."

He can't be serious, I thought. "Do you think that's all there is to it?"

"If you're lucky, yes. But in practice, no. What will Leclerc say?" Paul said.

"He won't object and I possess override authority if need be," I said. "But it'll be complicated to get it to Fredriksborg. Police and customs will be nervous now when the war is about to move into Acheron."

"Yes... I remember Manila. And now... Japanese marching into Acheron's villages." Paul fell silent. Both of us knew the implications.

I changed subject: "What about Adèle?"

Paul's shoulders slumped for a moment. "Last year she went to Karquim as a part of her graduate studies. But I've no idea what has happened to her when the Imperials attacked the city. She might be dead."

Paul's younger sister had been a temperamental and joyful adolescent at our last meeting. "I'm sorry. If I had known, I would have gotten in touch with her when we were there. We fled when we saw the Imperials planes coming in for the kill and we barely survived their bombing of the cloudport." I returned to my original question: "What are you doing here?"

"Thoughtless people have introduced European fish species in the Sea of Tears to increase catches. We're looking into the consequences. You know, such methods can be used for war. Disrupting farming with weeds or parasites," he said.

"It seems that Peter Lee was looking into that," I said.

"If he has a crop killer, he'll cause a famine across Acheron," said Paul.

"Well, volcanic ash is also a crop killer, isn't it?" I said. "And since he wanted to ignite Hephaestus Mons, he has no biological tricks up his sleeve."

"A plausible conclusion," said Paul. "Anyhow, I've decided that we'll head for Port Francis, an English settlement. You'll have to figure out how to proceed to Fredriksborg from there."

A sombre voice from the radio cut off our conversation: "We interrupt the music programme for an emergency news bulletin. Major general Lombardi, commander of Wehrkommando Alba in Neue Trieste, has announced that the battles on the southern ice sheet have ended. Last evening, colonel Nikefor Yefremovich Sokolov, commander of the 17th Caucasus Rifles, surrendered to major general Toshiro Miura, commander of the Japanese expeditionary corps in Alba. About one thousand Russian soldiers laid down their arms after two days fighting. The Habsburg Empire and the kingdom of Denmark-Norway remain neutral in this conflict and their governors have initiated talks on how to best protect their subjects' well-being in case the fighting reaches Acheron. Wehrkommando Alba has been ordered on full alert. All military personnel on leave shall at once report to their units. Long live Emperor Otto!" The voice fell silent and a military band started playing the Habsburg imperial hymn.

"The hurricane is about to strike." The words left a bitter taste in my mouth. I hated the notion of going into battle once again.

Paul's voice was equally strained: "Linda and you must hurry if you are to reach Fredriksborg before the Japanese invade."

Port Francis felt in part like a small newly-erected version of Fredriksborg and in part like a rural fishing village, where a breeze that carried a salty scent of seawater tugged at your clothes. The black log houses were lower, coarser and built without the Danes' strict symmetry. England's white flag with the red George cross fluttered over the customs house at the quay, but nobody came out to inspect the *Nereid*. On the other hand, research vessels rarely carry trading goods subject to custom duties.

From the bow Linda and I watched the *Nereid's* crew loading supplies and coal. On the quay behind us longshoremen unloaded black crates with fresh catches from fishing boats and whaleboats run by the men who hunt Alba's dugongs. Traders and skippers dickered at the warehouse gates.

"I have thought a lot about what we've seen and I want to tell you what I think. I would like to hear whether my conclusions match yours," I said to Linda. I had come to trust her common sense regardless of her lack of grounding in science.

"Mmm," she said.

"As for Peter Lee's leviathan tricks – pheromones are not easy to synthesize. He needs labs, assistants, raw material. Those things cost a lot. His employer must be wealthy," I said.

"I agree," said Linda.

"So we're talking about large-scale zoological research. Who would carry out that in Alba?" I said.

"Ask Yitzchak and Robert. They must know," she said.

"I'll do that," I said.

"What will you do when they tell you?" she asked.

"Nothing," I said.

Linda looked at me.

"You and I can't deal with every problem coming our way. Our job is to take that barrel to Fredriksborg. Captain Thorn's crew will have to deal with the biological warfare."

I wanted to charter a teamster who could take Linda, me and the barrel overland to Fredriksborg. Theoretically, the *Nereid* could have taken us to Neue Trieste, where there was a railway connection to Fredriksborg, but that city was well-organized by local standards and since the Emperor's army was mobilizing I did not look forward having to explain my doings to railway officials or customs officers. Port Francis ought to have people who would do the job with few questions asked.

Our tour of the town revealed that cargo transport was either by huge diesel-powered halftracks, who carried out long-distance assignments, or by bremmut, a big and sluggish herbivore that resembled a six-legged rhinoceros with a bull's head. That pack animal could take big loads over short distances at the speed of a walking man, whereas a halftrack could make ten knot on a decent gravel track.

Linda and I joined Paul, Robert and Yitzchak for lunch in the mess – time for an improvised war council.

"Linda has chartered a teamster," I said. "We're leaving in the afternoon for a halftrack journey to Fredriksborg."

"That's a long trip through the wilderness. I hope there aren't any other passengers," said Paul.

"Only the teamster Victor Szenes and his son and apprentice Jacob. I've done business with Mr Szenes before. I told that we are taking scientific samples to Fredriksborg and he accepted my story. He already knew that Johnny and I were aboard the *Nereid*," said Linda.

"You need more money now, don't you?" said Paul.

"Yes, I'd appreciate five thousand," I said. When we agreed on the charter, Szenes had asked for more money than what I had at hand, but we had agreed on a down payment in the garage, a first instalment on the quay and a second one in Fredriksborg.

"I'll fix that. When are they picking up the cargo?" Paul said.

"At two o'clock," I said.

"Good – you chaps will take care of that." Paul nodded at Robert and Yitzchak and changed subject. "Mr Bornewald, you said a while ago you had something else on you mind for the three of us."

I outlined Linda's and my thoughts about a conspiracy inside a research programme.

"Interesting, though hard to carry out. We have to check whether any of Peter Lee's old colleagues are in Alba. People that he would trust," Robert said.

Paul interrupted: "We'll set off for Neue Trieste tomorrow to check that."

Paul waited at the gangway when I was about to step off the *Nereid* for the last time. A stubborn wind from the Sea of Tears made him squint. "Johnny, I know you don't want to be armed." He carried a leather gun case in the right hand and a cardboard carton in the left. "But it is war now and you have a woman to protect. This is my Beretta Falcone and fifty cartridges buckshot."

"How would it help?" My backpack and the sailor's sack with fresh clothes that the *Nereid's* steward had handed over a moment ago were more than sufficient burdens.

"Remember Manila."

I understood his concern. "All right, for her sake."

"Bon voyage," he mumbled. "See you in Greifswald."

"If we meet again, we'll meet there." We who danced with the Grim Reaper – regardless whether we were conscripted Russian peasants or aristocratic Swedish volunteers – would not be able to dodge his scythe forever. Cats have nine lives, the proverb says, but men don't; Paul and I would probably never meet again.

I took the pump-action gun and the ammunition and walked slowly down the swaying gangway to the stone-paved quay. The halftrack, a worn blue Hercule Autochenille from Fabrique Royale des Camions in Lyons, waited tall as a house in front of me. A stylized black monster head glared at me from above the windshield. On the flatbed a tarpaulin covered our barrel together with half a dozen fuel barrels. The diesel engine thudded and vertical exhaust pipes behind the cab puffed stinking smoke.

Yitzchak, who had assisted the teamsters when the *Nereid's* crane transferred the barrel, stood next to the cab and chatted with Victor Szenes who leaned out of the window. Their Yiddish was so colloquial that I barely understood a word.

I looked back at the ship. Linda walked down the gangway, dressed in a navy blue sailor's jacket, a black turtleneck sweater and a brown knitted cap. Someone had cut her hair so short that not a strand was visible. All pieces of clothing were too big, so she looked like a schoolboy dressed in his father's work clothes. She carried the same type of sailor's sack as I did. "Call me Connor," she said in a light tone. "Sometimes it's better to be a bloke."

"For sure," I said.

A quick farewell to Yitzchak and then we climbed into the cab, six feet above the ground, through the right door. I saw the vehicle's name painted in blackletter script above it: Behemoth.

The cab seat was a sofa wide enough for four adult males. With two slim people in the middle, nobody would feel cramped. I put our luggage behind the seat. There I found a gun rack with a twin-barrelled shotgun and an old French army rifle. A sleeper with a narrow bunk bed at the cab's rear would provide rest at stops in the wilderness.

Victor Szenes disregarded Linda's new clothes, saying merely: "Are you ready?" as he put a checked cloth cap on his bald pate. I nodded and handed him the first instalment of his fee. He put away the coin rolls without counting.

Jacob Szenes, on the other hand, paid a lot of attention to Linda, but he said nothing. A pimple-faced teenage boy in a brown leather jacket and black denim trousers next to an oddly dressed woman – well, I had been a youngster, too, before the rebellion.

The teamster made a thumbs-up gesture at Yitzchak, closed the window to his left and moved the gear stick. The Behemoth rumbled forward, its tracks scratching white scars in the stone pavement.

Thus the last stage of our Alban odyssey began. I glimpsed the journey's end but did not feel relieved. Too much had gone wrong already.

CHAPTER 17

One hour after departure the mercury barometer on Behemoth's dashboard had fallen one inch. The sun vanished behind a thick layer of grey clouds. The wind turned to the southwest and gained in force. The cab was poorly insulated so we had to put on extra clothes to stay warm. Victor Szenes passed around a thermos flask with coffee. The crackling radio tuned to Radio Austria International was barely audible above the engine noise.

Acheron is a bowl in Alba's surface, but it is so gigantic that you cannot perceive its curvature with the naked eye. The halftrack rumbled across a plain divided in broad fields. The local crop resembled sweet corn, but it was black like most native plants: acre after acre of six-foot swaying stalks extending on both sides of the gravel track, creating a scene more appropriate for Hades than for Earth. The low brown farmhouses were the sole contrast to the ever-present black. The ursines' farming technology was old-fashioned with bremmuts harnessed to most heavy machinery. The quadruped farmhands looked at us when Behemoth rumbled by, but resumed working almost at once.

During the afternoon the rain increased from occasional splashes to a downpour. Victor Szenes switched on a strong headlight, whose cone of light penetrated ten-fifteen yards into the rain, and drove on without much concern. After all, this was his home turf and he probably knew every inch of the route.

After six hours on the road and in pitch darkness Behemoth drove into a yard next to a broad building and stopped. There was not a person to be seen: everyone had taken refuge indoors from the weather. The headlight illuminated a metal signboard in the traditional English style above the entrance: a white five-pointed star on a green background. The White Star

Inn had been designed by humans for humans, even though its builders had used the local black wood and brown stone. I saw a stable to the left and a broad carport with three walls to the right. The halftrack was too tall to fit under its roof.

"Good food." I put down the knife and fork on the plate in front of me. The belly was filled by well-spiced beef and mediocre beer and I felt ready to doze off.

"We often stay here during long hauls," said Victor and exhaled a cloud of acrid cigarillo smoke. "Good food and the beds are comfortable."

The dining room was almost empty. My eyes wandered among the prints of English hunting scenes on the light green wall panels, an enlivening contrast against the black wooden furniture and the black firewood in the hearth. I guessed that the innkeeper aspired to the ambience of a European inn, but with little success. There were few guests here for the night, and the receptionist had offered me a discount when I requested three rooms instead of the two he had expected.

Someone opened the inn's front door with excessive force. I glanced at the door to the reception. It swung open and three soldiers entered, two privates and one corporal in Imperial grey. The uniforms were unkempt and the boots mud-splatted. They tossed their rifles on a bench.

"Fräulein, bitte essen," the corporal called at the serving maid. His voice was slurred from alcohol and he spoke German with an accent I could not place. After all, emperor Otto ruled over a score Central European peoples. The trio sat down at a table while the serving maid approached with the menu. The men discussed it in lively voices.

"They're Poles," whispered Linda.

"Do you understand what they say?" I asked.

"Not much. But they're drunk," she said.

"Drunk on duty. I wonder how their sergeant will deal with that," I said.

One of the privates got up and walked toward us in a reasonably steady gait. He glared at Victor, who stared back with a firm gaze.

"Who're you?" the soldier said in poor German. His furrowed face was pale with shadows around the eyes. This teenager had seen more than a youngster should.

"Travellers," I said in the same language.

"I didn't speak to you, garçon. I spoke to the old man there."

"Travellers," said Victor. His face showed no feelings, no thoughts.

"So that's your truck ou' there?" said the soldier?

Victor nodded.

"It's wa' now. The Emperor's army needs it, old man." The soldier leaned over us. His breath reeked of cheap vodka.

Victor shook his head slowly. "The army doesn't do requisitions in that way."

"Listen here, żyd. We need your truck and we don't give a fuck what you think." The soldier raised his right hand. Victor rose out of his chair in one swift movement that sent plates, wineglasses and cutlery tumbling over the white tablecloth. He caught the soldier's descending arm at the wrist and twisted it sidewise downward. The soldier groaned with pain while bending forward. His buddies got up and grabbed their rifles. The waitress fled screaming into the kitchen.

"Old man, let go!" shouted the corporal. Victor obeyed; no sane person argues with a raised gun barrel.

The private staggered backwards. Jacob sat completely still and watched the other Poles.

"Fucking troublemakers," said the corporal. He gave an order in Polish. The quarrelsome private returned to his seat, but before he had arrived, the corporal stepped forward and punched him hard in solar plexus. The private collapsed in a moaning heap on the floor.

The innkeeper, a thin elderly man in a black suit, came out from the kitchen and stopped. He looked amiss at the situation.

The corporal put his rifle on the table next to him. "Gentlemen, I apologize for my man's loutish behaviour. The Imperial army does not requisition civilian possessions in this manner," he said.

Victor responded by a reserved nod. "I know. Apology accepted."

The fallen soldier got back on his feet.

The innkeeper headed for our table. "Gentlemen, this is embarrassing." His face was pale and the mouth a tense narrow line.

"Not your fault, Herr Lothari. The times are bad," said Victor.

"Herr Szenes, you have often been a welcome guest." Lothari rubbed his palms together.

"Considering the food Johann and Erika serve at every visit, I'll keep on staying here when my job takes me this way." During our meal Victor Szenes had joked with the middle-aged waitress in a manner that showed that he was a regular customer.

"We'll retire now," I said.

Linda walked near me when we exited the dining room and I glimpsed in the corner of my eye how the quarrelsome soldier made a lewd gesture at us.

When we passed through the hallway, a maid walked by, her arms burdened by bed linen.

I addressed her: "Fräulein, those three soldiers. How did they arrive?"

"They came on foot, sir."

Her answer confirmed my suspicions. "Thank you, Fräulein." Now we had to act swiftly before matters got out hand. I followed Linda up the stair to the second floor and entered her room. After closing the door, I said: "Those soldiers, they're probably deserters."

"Why do you think so?" said Linda.

"Soldiers don't move around in civilian areas in small teams like that. If they had been ten or twenty privates with a sergeant in charge, I wouldn't be suspicious. Also, they're drunk and unkempt. I think they're planning to steal the halftrack tonight. They want to leave Imperial territory as fast as possible. You and I must stop them," I said.

Linda nodded.

I continued: "If the barrel hadn't been on the flatbed, I wouldn't have bothered with them."

"You're right. Now let's get moving," said Linda and opened the tiny room's sole window. It looked out over the inn's rear side. The only illumination came from kerosene lamps inside the main building's room facing this way. Linda pulled a waterproof poncho and a torchlight from her bag. I had to endure the rain without protection.

The ground was ten feet away so it was an easy task lowering Linda. I climbed down and then we walked between garbage bins, shed and a henhouse across the backyard.

When we arrived at Behemoth's left front wheel next to the empty carport, I took the auto-picklock from my jacket pocket and used it to open the door and sneak into the rear of the cab. I broke open the carton of buckshot and crammed several cartridges into my pockets. Then I took Paul's Beretta and handed the other shotgun to Linda.

We climbed on top of the carport to wait in the pouring rain: minute after minute of cold misery on its corrugated tin roof. Clouds covered the night sky, so the passage of time could not be determined by the movements of the moon and the stars.

The inn's main entrance opened and I saw three people silhouetted against the interior lights. One carried a kerosene lamp. They walked in the unsteady gait of men that had fortified their courage with vodka and beer. Even if they managed to steal the halftrack, they would have trouble keeping a steady course along the local dirt tracks.

Two soldiers entered the carport to seek protection from the rain. None checked the roof where Linda and I huddled. The third soldier approached the halftrack, put the lantern on the ground next to the cab door facing us and leaned his rifle against the vehicle. Metal croaked when he tried to pry the door open with his bayonet.

I hardened my mind, entering a killer mode. War is dishonourable business – one prefers to ambush unprepared opponents. Without a sound I slid down in the cover of the carport's rear wall, out of sight from the halftrack behind a corner. Four quick steps took me to the prospective burglar. He turned toward me during the dash, fumbling for his rifle. My rifle butt struck his groin and he toppled with a scream.

I retreated halfway around the corner and raised the Beretta in firing position. The two soldiers came around the corner into the lantern light, their rifles ready with bayonets in place.

Linda fired; two dry sharp cracks from the carport roof. Two shotgun blasts tore through the chests of two young men. Death took them before they realized who had shot. The transuranium bomb reaped new victims.

The surviving Pole screamed wordlessly into the dark. He tried to get up but failed.

"Are you going to kill him?" said Linda in English from somewhere above my head.

"No. Let him live. He won't understand anything," I said.

I walked into the lantern light with my shotgun aimed at the survivor's face and kicked his rifle out of his reach. He crawled backward to the halftrack and used it as support when getting up on his feet.

"Flee!" I said in German. "You live."

Crying and snivelling he staggered into the rain and the darkness. I did not see in what direction he fled and I never found out what became of him.

I hobbled in under the carport's roof and sat down on its earth floor. My hands trembled. Linda soon joined me. Someone called from the main building and I responded by shouting: "Help us!"

Victor Szenes and a handyman came after a while. They carried kerosene lanterns that partially dispersed darkness but that also made them excellent targets. Their questions turned into meaningless noise, but they guided us back into light and warmth.

Lothari's staff put us in easy chairs in front of the open fire in the tap room and fetched dry clothes and hot cocoa. The innkeeper hovered at the edge of my field of vision with a shotgun in his hands. He and Victor talked with one another, but I ignored them. My inner eye showed only the death of two young Poles again and again.

"Herr Bornewald, two policemen have come to talk to you." Lothari's voice dispelled the shadows in my mind for a moment.

My watch said that two and a half hour had passed since the firefight. I had not moved from my easy chair. "I'm coming."

Linda looked at me, but did not move.

"I'll send for you if need be," I said.

"I don't want to talk to the police." Her voice was weak and flat.

Lothari guided me to a small office, where two sombre men waited, one in a grey business suit and one in a blue field uniform.

The civilian shook my hand with a firm grip. "Good evening, I am detective sergeant Conti of the Criminal Investigation Service and this is lieutenant Schreiber of the Imperial Gendarmerie." His dialect indicated that he was born in Vienna. Schreiber raised his hand in a military salute.

"I'm Johnny Bornewald." I focused my mind on the ordeal ahead of me. During the past hour I had rehearsed in my mind what to say in a police interrogation.

"Let's sit down and talk this through this matter." Conti gestured at three simple chairs and turned to Lothari. "Thanks for the help. We will call for you if we need further assistance."

Lothari left, closing the door gently behind him.

"Well, Herr Bornewald, who are you?" Conti's voice was calm, a professional doing his job.

"I'm a travelling agent for the cloudship *Cassiopeia*, which currently is undergoing repairs in Fredriksborg's cloudport. Miss Connor is my guide. We have been looking around for trade goods that the captain could sell in Magalhana for a profit."

Schreiber jotted down every word I said in his notebook.

"Why do you travel in an empty halftrack?" said Conti.

"The trip has been unsuccessful. In Port Francis, we heard the news of the Imperial mobilization. I decided to return to Fredriksborg at once to avoid getting stranded in the wilderness in case of a full-scale war. I charted Victor Szenes to take us there," I said.

"What happened when the two men died?" said Conti.

I let my inner darkness tint my voice: "I got suspicious when I saw the men enter the dining room. Drunken louts in uniform. One of them threatened Herr Szenes, demanding to 'requisition' the halftrack. I assumed the soldiers were deserters on the run. We had some valuables in the halftrack, so after our meal I decided to go and get them so that they would not be stolen during the night. Miss Connor came along. When we were at the halftrack, the soldiers left the inn. They seemed to be more intoxicated so I worried what they might be up to. I grabbed a shotgun from the halftrack to protect Miss Connor. The soldiers came up to us and behaved like pigs. When they started fumbling with the rifles, I fired two rounds because I was convinced they intended to bayonet me and rape Miss Connor. Two fell, while the third escaped into the darkness. I have no idea what happened to him."

"Did you consider any less violent course of action?" asked Conti.

"Three drunken aggressive soldiers with rifles? No, I did not. I wanted to protect us," I said.

"Do you think Miss Connor has anything to add to your statement?" asked Conti.

"No, I don't think so," I said.

"Your account matches statements made by Herr Lothari and Herr Szenes. I will write a report on the event tomorrow where I will explain that the killings are to be considered justified self-defence. And you made the right assumption, Herr Bornewald. Those men were deserters from the Imperial army." Conti rose from the chair and his neutral facial expression changed to a look of genuine concern. "We will leave you now. May your continued journey to Fredriksborg be spared of more misery."

I shook the policemen's hands and walked back to Linda in the tap room.

Just after dawn Behemoth took us away from the White Star Inn. The rain had stopped, but clouds still covered the sky. My eyes felt like they were full of grit. I hadn't slept much, because whenever I dozed off, nightmares appeared. Linda looked like she had had a similar night and now she slumbered uneasily next to me. I gazed through the windshield at the never-ending black fields.

I glimpsed an even darker shadow at the horizon. "What's that far ahead?"

"The Iron Wood," said Jacob, "and we're going through it. It'll take a few hours. Many dirt tracks cross it."

The shadow grew into a band that turned into a forest that stretched left and right as far as I could see. Victor Szenes drove along the trail into arboreal gloom. Bare trunks rose like ebony pillars for twenty yards and then flared into brushy coniferous umbrellas. I pondered on what kind of herd animals had cleared this trail over long years. Behemoth's speed fell to eight knots on the rough ground. Grazing spidery animals, the size of big rats, fled from the clamouring steel giant through the bountiful dark undergrowth.

"Food break!" Victor Szenes stopped Behemoth in a glade. I climbed out of the cab. The sky was grey, and the forest seemed to cloud our surroundings with layers of shadow. A cold moist breeze carried a bitter scent, probably from the trees etheric oils.

"Johnny, I'm sick," said Linda huddled on the seat. "I must lie down."

"Do so," I said. "Sleep while Mr Szenes and I prepare the food."

She got into a bunk in the cab's rear and vanished under a blanket.

Jacob, holding a hatchet, walked away into the silent shadows to get firewood. Old dry needles crackled under his soles.

Victor Szenes and I unloaded a field stove with accoutrements from a cargo box underneath Behemoth's body. When everything was ready for cooking a meal, he broke the silence: "Herr Bornewald, before we left Port Francis, Yitzchak Asimoff told me how you and he had met many years ago in Europe." He made a brief pause. "I can't understand how man with those qualities walks into the night and kills two drunken youngsters just to prevent them from stealing my halftrack. You don't seem cold-hearted enough to value property above human lives."

I gazed at the black trees. I did not want to face Victor Szenes's weary eyes; I did not want to explain myself. The wind shook the brushy branches. Two spider squirrels watched me with multiple eyes. Jacob's hatchet chopped wood nearby, but I could not see him among the shadows. "No, I am no icy killer. Something big is at stake, so big that I had to shoot them."

"What is at stake?" he said.

"Are you sure that you want to learn that? It is a risky matter," I said.

"Maybe not everything, but I want to understand what I have got entangled in. My son's life is at stake," he said.

I acquiesced, because I wanted to act honourably. "I am not the person I claim to be."

"Herr Asimoff explained that. It is solely his account for what you did for those refugees that has convinced me to continue travelling with you after last night's events."

"I am a republican activist. I struggle for world that offers more freedom to all people. I am an aristocrat, but I reject the elites' despotism." I interrupted the harangue, because I realized it sounded sentimental.

"The cargo I transport, is it hazardous?" said Victor Szenes.

"Yes and no. No immediate hazard to anyone. But it is Pandora's box. If it is ever used, the world will not remain the same. People simply must not steal it."

"Is it something that can end the war with a republican victory?" he said.

"No, it isn't that easy. The war is like a wildfire, unstoppable, uncontrollable. But whoever knows what Pandora's box contains, can use that knowledge to his advantage. I want to give that knowledge to the republics."

"I am a simple man, earning a living for my family by transporting goods in the wilderness. By what right do you involve me in your war?" he said.

"There is not such right. This barrel is so important that I must get it off Alba as fast as I can," I said.

"You're not treating us fairly," he said.

"No, I don't. War is not fair. Pestilence and famine walk behind the advancing armies. An individual can only try to do what is right," I said.

"Involving Jacob was wrong. He is too young," he said.

Those words hurt like a slap to the cheek. "I am sorry. Poor judgment by me."

Unexpectedly Victor Szenes put his hand on my right shoulder. I turned my head to look into his face. He said: "Young man, in Rome you can see the Titus Arch, raised by an emperor to glorify the destruction of our temple in Jerusalem. The Romans also tortured your master to death. I, a Jew, and you, a Christian, stand here nineteen hundred years later whereas that empire is only rubble. Tyrants may kill individuals that stand up against them, but good ideas sown by such people will nevertheless survive. But if you start to resemble your enemy, Rome has defeated you."

I did not know what to say. I had gone astray and now I faced it.

Victor smiled grimly: "Go on fighting, sir Percival." He fetched a smoke lamb leg from a grocery box and started to slice it.

CHAPTER 18

"Fredriksborg ahoy!" Jacob Szenes stretched an arm past Linda and nudged me. The colourful dreams dissolved without a trace and I noticed that Behemoth still followed the broad gravel roads we had reached when exiting the Iron Wood. The Danish city glittered faintly at an indeterminate distance in the night and dispelled some of the darkness in my mind. I understood why Xenophon's men had shouted joyfully when glimpsing the Black Sea after their long march through the Anatolian mountains. Soon I would be among friends.

"Less than an hour remaining," said Victor Szenes.

I switched on the radio and tuned in the city's Danish-language broadcast. An organ played in the crackling loudspeaker, evening service at Sankt Knud's Lutheran church. Just after the final hymn had concluded, Behemoth reached the town's edge. It headlight illuminated a sturdy boom, striped in white and red, that blocked the road. It was accompanied on both sides by iron hedgehogs wrapped in barbed wire. The Danish army had also built several firing positions around the gate.

A black guardhouse was located next to the boom. Two policemen with cavalry carbines came out and checked Behemoth's exterior with their torchlights. Victor Szenes opened the cab window and addressed them in German: "Constable Riise, good evening."

"Herr Szenes, welcome back. What's your cargo today?" The Danish accent made Riise's German hard to understand.

"Only two stranded cloudmen returning to their ship."

"Tell them to come down. I want to talk to them," said the policeman.

Linda and I climbed down to the ground. A machine gun crew pointed a thick water-cooled barrel at us through the sand bags of their strongpoint.

Riise's torchlight blinded us as he inspected our faces. "Who are you?" he said in German.

"I am Johnny Bornewald and this is my guide Linda Connor. I am a travelling trade agent from the cloudship *Cassiopeia* which currently should be in your cloudport," I explained.

"Yes, I know her. Stranded with engine troubles," said Riise.

"I have been around looking for goods to take to Magalhana. When we were in Port Francis, the news on the radio mentioned that the risk of war had increased, so I decided to get back to the ship. I chartered Herr Szenes to drive us here," I said.

"Any goods to declare," asked the policeman.

"No," I said.

"Your travel documents, please."

I handed them over, as did Linda. Riise positioned himself in the cone from Behemoth's headlight and started to read them. Meanwhile, his colleague headed for the rear of the halftrack. The tarpaulin rustled when he pulled it aside. "There are just fuel barrels here, sergeant," he called. His native language must have been Icelandic, because his Danish sounded almost like Swedish.

"Just a moment, Herr Bornewald. I have to make a phone call," said Riise and headed for the guardhouse with our travel documents.

I checked the surroundings while waiting. The soldiers appeared to be alert but not tense. The Icelandic policeman spent more time glancing at Linda's behind that watching me or Behemoth. So the Danes perceived no imminent risk of war.

Five minutes later, Riise returned. "I've talked to Willem Laan in the *Cassiopeia*. He's happy that you have returned safe and sound. Welcome to Fredriksborg." He signalled to the nearest soldiers to raise the boom.

We climbed into the cab and Behemoth moved forward. I sighed with relief: back in safety. One problem remained, however: how to get our barrel past the customs officers at the cloudport.

"Where do you want to go?" asked Victor Szenes.

"Would it be possible for you to park Behemoth in a secure place while Linda and I walk to the *Cassiopeia* to settle the final details with captain Leclerc? He's the one who decides how we're going to get that thing to the ship," I said.

"My cousin has a workshop near the cloudport. We'll go there," said Victor Szenes. He navigated the huge halftrack smoothly through the narrow streets of Fredriksborg and after a few minutes we arrived at a steel gate with barbed wire along the top. Beyond it I glimpsed a large yard, containing lorries, cars and aeroplanes in varying states of disrepair, adjoined by a two-story stone building adorned with a sign saying *Szenes Mekanik A/S*. Electrical lamps gleamed behind three windows on its top floor. Behemoth's klaxon howled – two short, one long. While we waited, I scanned the surroundings: across the street a carpentry workshop, to the right a painter's shop. This must be a district for artisans and tradesmen.

The gate swung inwards, opened by a young woman in an overall. I recognized her: she had driven a lorry past the cloudport customs office during my first hour in Fredriksborg. She waved a welcome at the cab when the Behemoth into the yard and parked. We dismounted and Victor Szenes hugged the woman. They conversed in an unknown language that I presumed to be Hungarian.

"This is my niece Hannah." Victor Szenes made the introduction in German. "The family is big. Hannah is our troubadour."

I shook her hand: "Pleased to meet you. I'm Johnny Bornewald."

"Welcome." Hannah Szenes spoke flawless German. "I already know Miss Connor. She has done some jobs for us here in the garage."

Linda nodded.

I turned to Victor Szenes and handed over the last part of our fare. "Thanks for a safe journey. I'm leaving the Beretta in your gun rack for the time being."

"All right. That's all for tonight then," said Victor Szenes. "Follow the wide street to your right and you'll soon reach the cloudport's main gate. See you here tomorrow."

We walked for two blocks and entered Fredriksborg's red-light district. All ports – no matter whether they serve the oceans or the sky – attract the same types of seedy establishments. Loud bouncers outside bars and gambling dens competed for attention. Drunkards staggered in side alleys and vomited behind toppled garbage bins.

"Hi, sailor boy!" The woman who called for my attention from a window on the second floor had grotesque make-up in pink and lilac. The lacy dress revealed a disgusting amount of bulging flesh. "I can give you more fun than that little nancy-boy." She spoke English with a heavy Danish accent.

Linda shouted at her in Russian, a long harangue where I only deciphered one word: *prostitutka*.

The harlot smirked: "Pažalsta, there is space for you too in my bed. It's wide, unlike your arse."

Linda showed her the finger, clenched the jaws and trudged on in silence next to me.

Three blocks later we arrived at the cloudport's gate. Willem Laan waited in the light from a solitary street lamp next to the guard post.

"Wonderful to see you again. Are you well? We feared that you had died up on the ice."

"We are fine. Let's talk about the rest on board," I said.

Willem nodded: "Captain Leclerc is waiting."

The guard on duty let us in through the gate without further ado.

Four cups of steaming coffee waited for us on Leclerc's desk. He greeted us in German: "Welcome home, both of you. I thought the war had killed you." Leclerc rarely showed much emotion, but tonight his voice sounded joyful. He waved at the cups. Some ash fell from the tip of his smouldering cigarillo and sullied the deck. "I tried to use your infernal device, Johnny, but the stuff probably isn't as bitter as you want it. Get seated, please."

"Thanks, captain," I said.

"Something else with the coffee? Cognac? Liqueur?" the captain asked.

Linda shook her head.

"No thanks," I said. "But I'd like some sandwiches."

Leclerc looked at Willem: "Fix that, please." Willem left for the mess.

I took a big sip and felt pleasure of the caffeine entering my system. "A good brew, captain."

Leclerc nodded. "Thanks. Now, please, give me a summary of your adventures."

"Miss Connor knows what's going on," I said and switched to badly accented Dutch: "Kolonel Ter Horst groet u en zegt dat zwarte adelaars naar de Rijn vliegen." The Inlichtendienst's current code phrase for "imminent war in Alba".

Leclerc gazed firmly at me: "Maurits van Oranje staat altijd klaar om ze in hun vlucht neer te schieten."

"Twaalf twintig dertien."

"Begrepen." Leclerc switched to German: "The writing has been on the wall for some days and now you've confirmed it. Well, the colonel knows that I'm ready for action."

"Do you want the complete story?" I said.

"No. If we get captured after the fighting starts, I might get tortured. So give me a judicious summary," he said.

However, the summary turned out quite long. When Willem returned with our sandwiches, Leclerc dismissed him for "security reasons". As I approached the end of my story, I refrained from explaining what Pandora's Box contained.

When I eventually fell silent, Leclerc said: "You chaps seem to have more lives than a cat."

His words let loose dark thoughts in my mind: *Cats, bloody hell no! We've survived by leaving a trail of death behind us. War creates only killers and corpses.*

Leclerc leaned back and grabbed a sandwich. "Johnny, you have to find a way of getting that box on board discreetly. The customs people have tightened their checks during the last few days, after the Russians lost to the Japanese on the ice sheet."

"I know. Let me sleep for a night and I'll come up with a scheme," I said.

"All right. I'll tell Willem to move into the forecastle for the time being. You two need a chance to sleep in peace," said Leclerc.

"Johnny, are you awake?" Linda whispered from my bunk.

I turned in discomfort in Willem's bunk. Sleep eluded me. Bloodcurdling scenes from our journey ran in a loop for my inner eyes. The cabin, my only home in a messy world, provided no relief, despite its familiar smells and background sounds. "Mmm, I'm listening."

"Why do you keep Leclerc in the dark?" said Linda. "That colonel you spoke of is not your true boss."

"Well, Ter Horst and the Institute work together quite often. It was the colonel who got me aboard this ship. I prefer to appeal to the captain's foremost loyalties, to his sovereign and his country," I said.

"So the Netherlands is no republic?" she said.

"Well, half-way a republic, perhaps. But the Institute can't be too picky about its friends in this war," I said.

After a long silence Linda said: "What do you think you will say about that in 1945?"

"I don't know." The question guided my thoughts in a new direction: *No war lasts forever. What will the samurai do when peace arrives? Put his katana on the wall above the fireplace?*

.

CHAPTER 19

"Willem, have you dealt with the customs office during my absence?" An invigorating aroma permeated the mess as I brewed my morning coffee; what a delight to handle the dark powder once again.

He munched a sandwich while answering: "A few times. They've tightened up everything the last few days. They work in teams and appear to fear sabotage. After all, the military airfield is next door." He turned to Linda who was eating oatmeal porridge with applesauce. "Miss Connor, if you wait for half an hour after breakfast, I'll provide you with employment documents. Captain has given green light for signing you on as a cloudman. What Christian name do you want?"

"What?" Linda looked puzzled.

"We can't have a woman in the crew. No one would believe it. You must be disguised as a lad," said Willem.

"Leonard'll be all right," said Linda. She obviously had not heard of European cloudmen's prejudices against having women aboard.

One hour later, Linda and I left the *Cassiopeia*. I wanted to study the routines of the customs officers. Soldiers patrolled the tarmac and manned machine-gun positions here and there. Those guns were mounted to be able to fire at aircraft as well as ground targets. When we walked past the customs office, I saw that there were three officers on duty instead of one.

"I think the best scheme is to hide our object inside Behemoth's body, not on the flatbed. Then we let Szenes take legitimate cargo to the *Cassiopeia*. The customs people will check that, but they'll hardly suspect Victor Szenes for any shenanigans because he ought to be well known to them. What do you think?" I asked.

110

"It might work, as long as they aren't very diligent," said Linda.

"They have no reason to suspect that we are smuggling anything out of Fredriksborg. They and the military are probably more worried about sabotage to the cloudport and airfield," I said.

A dozen machine guns opened fire behind us. Their hellish racket sent Linda and me tumbling into cover under a nearby truck. I pulled the binocular out of my backpack and scanned the sky. Far above us an aeroplane moved in a wide circle, well beyond the range of the machine guns. The gyro started whirring to compensate for my trembling hands when I zoomed in on the aircraft: a monoplane with red wing roundels. "Japanese photo reconnaissance," I said.

Engines roared in the vicinity and I shifted my attention to them. Two fighter biplanes with the Danish flag on the tailfins climbed sharply from the military airfield. "Those planes can't get close to that Jap," I said. "Let's move on, shall we."

Linda nodded and got up from the asphalt.

When we arrived at the Szenes's workshop after walking through the littered and currently quiet bar district, I once again scanned the sky with my binocular. The Danish fighters were circling in figures of eight more than ten thousand feet above us. The Japanese monoplane cruised slowly at a much higher altitude, out of range from their machine guns. Its cameras were probably busy clicking away. Many people in the vicinity had stopped working to look at the events in the sky.

We entered the workshop through the main entrance. As soon as I had opened the door, I heard the raspy voice of an old man speaking in Danish on the radio in a nearby room. While we walked on, I gave Linda a simultaneous summary in English.

"... are ready to defend the subjects and territories of the Danish Crown in Alba. We have not yet been able to determine whether the Japanese also have attacked our king's possessions in Europe, Asia or Magalhana. Today I have proclaimed martial law and thereby authorized general Rantzau to carry out whatever defensive measures he deems necessary. Civilian property can now be requisitioned by the military. All male subjects between fourteen and sixty years of age may be drafted to labour companies by the military and civilian county administrators. Unrest, sedition and subversion will be punished according the war paragraphs in the penal code. The police have received extraordinary authority to act against anyone obstructing the war efforts. Looters and rioters will be shot. Troubled times are ahead of us. It is only through disciplined behaviour and hard work that we will be able to fend off this assault on our homes and our honour. Long live King Christian!" A military band started playing the Danish royal anthem *Kong Christian stod vid højen mast.*

In the building's common room Victor, Jacob, Hannah and middle-aged man in a mechanic's overall sat next to a large radio in a piece of teak furniture.

"Good morning," Victor Szenes said in German. "The Japanese have attacked Christianshus. That was governor Trampe speaking to the people."

Another voice from the radio cut him off: "There will be news broadcasts on top of every hour for the rest of the day and ongoing programs will be interrupted for urgent bulletins. Regular programming is cancelled until further notice. We will now play *Messiah* by Händel in a recording from 1932, performed by the Copenhagen Symphony Orchestra and the Roskilde Cathedral Choir. Conductor is Jan Toll." Hannah Szenes turned down the volume to a mild background noise.

Victor Szenes introduced the stranger: "This is Daniel Szenes, the owner of the workshop and Hannah's uncle."

Daniel addressed Linda in slow Yiddish: "Welcome back." Then he turned to me: "Herr Bornewald, you are a travelled man they tell me. I left Europe long ago and have never bothered with the doings of kings and emperors in faraway lands. But now their wars have come to Alba. What can you tell me about the Japanese?"

I answered in German: "Aggressive and expansionist. They have fought many wars against China, Russia, Mexico and Spain. Their soldiers are feared everywhere around the Pacific Ocean. They are taking no risks by attacking Danish territory here, because Denmark cannot threaten Japan's home islands."

"Will general Rantzau's army be able to stop them?" said Daniel.

"I doubt that." I looked at Linda and then at Hannah and recalled the reports I had read in the Hamburger Handelszeitung about Japanese atrocities in the Philippines. The blood left my face and my legs trembled. "Where is the outhouse?" I mumbled.

"At the rear of the yard, next to the aeroplanes," said Daniel Szenes.

I walked away alone, every step feeling like a mile. *If my concentration falters, I will stumble and fall.* Outside the building I gazed at the blue sky and the distant Japanese aircraft. I lifted my hands into my field of vision. *The power over life and death,* I thought and closed my eyes. *Why am I the one to decide who will live, who will die?* My brother Abel's words rose out of some crevasse in my mind: "Privileges always entail matching duties." *Regardless what path I choose, children will lose their fathers and woman their husbands. Regardless where I go in the future, I will always carry the memory of what I did or did not do here.*

I turned inward in search of an answer. Anguish, glittering and burning like molten metal, filled my skull and the surroundings faded away. Suddenly I broke its choke-hold, took a deep breath and gazed into the core of my being. *Honour will be my succour: to protect women and children, to defend the weak.* I saw my path ahead, the path of death leading through darkness and fire. I opened my eyes. *May my courage stay firm till the bitter end.* I looked at the disassembled aeroplanes parked in the enclosed yard and decided: *That'll be the way.*

I returned indoors. "Ladies and gentlemen! I have changed my plans and I need your help." Two women, two men and one boy looked at me. "It falls on my shoulders to save Acheron from Japan's soldiers, but I can't accomplish that on my own."

"Will you use Pandora's box?" Linda forced those words out of her mouth with visible effort.

"Yes!" I said.

"I don't understand," said Victor Szenes.

"Sodom and Gomorrah," I said. "I will recreate Sodom and Gomorrah at Christianshus." Surtr the Fire Giant was hardly a mythological reference that Jews would recognize. "Fire and brimstone falling out of the sky."

"You're crazy," said Jacob Szenes.

"Doesn't matter," I said. "Do you want your cousin to be raped by Japanese soldiers?"

Jacob looked away from me. Hannah's face turned pale. She opened her mouth but no words came out.

"Johnny, do it!" Linda's voice had turned into a faint hissing. "Burn them to hell!"

Her words erased any hesitation remaining in my mind. "That happened in Manila six years ago. It won't happen again," I said.

"Explain what you mean," said Victor Szenes.

"Pandora's box contains the most powerful bomb ever made. I will use it to wipe out the Japanese force besieging Christianshus."

"But then you'll be killing Danish soldiers, too, won't you?" said Daniel Szenes.

"True. But what choice do we have? The Japanese will show no mercy to the vanquished," I said.

"I know," said Victor Szenes. "And I see how you think. You want to destroy the Japanese corps when it concentrated in one spot."

"That's right," I said.

"How the hell will you get that bomb to Christianshus? It far off and the Danes will hardly assist you," said Daniel Szenes.

"You'll make me a flyable aircraft from those fuselages in your yard," I said.

Five people looked at me in silence. *They must be thinking that I am out of my mind.*

"That can be done," said Daniel Szenes. "We have the right engines in the garage. But, Herr Bornewald, we need a lot of cash right away for spare parts."

"I have plenty of silver at hand. Can you finish the job by tomorrow evening?" I said.

"That'll be hard if you want to fly safely," said Daniel Szenes.

"I have some drugs that can keep you working through the night," I said.

"Herr Bornewald, how will you be able to fly that far? It'll be night and very cold," said Hannah Szenes.

"I'll take some pills to increase my endurance and sharpen my eyesight. Navigation will be easy because I'll follow the railroad all the way," I said.

"No time to lose," said Victor Szenes. "Let's start at once." He walked out of the room with a firm stride.

"Miss Szenes, try to get hold of a parachute. I need one to slow the bomb's descent," I said.

The next thirty-six hours whirled by without a break. Jacob Szenes and I cooked food and handled other logistical matters, while the others made me an aeroplane. Linda handled the bomb barrel by herself, an arrangement appreciated by the others. The mechanics' skilled hands attached wings made of wooden slats to a fuselage made from steel rods and covered the skeleton with fabric. The three men treated the two females with professional respect, whereas a woman in a European workshop would have been ridiculed. I approved of the rustic equality in the Alban mind-set.

I refrained from using Maxidin because I wanted a solid night's sleep. I would stuff myself with drugs the next night, so I did not want to weary my mind and body unnecessarily. However, worry foiled those plans. My body would not relax: soon I would kill thousands. I wished time and time again that I would be spared from doing this deed, but no.

The radio provided continuous music and war news. Fighting raged around the fortifications at Christianshus and the Danes appeared to be the weaker party. The authorities in Fredriksborg mobilized society by instituting rationing, curfew, black-out and so on.

I visited captain Leclerc in the *Cassiopeia* and explained summarily that I had to go away again. On the way back, I bought a set of maps for Acheron in a bookshop. The route to Christianshus curved around Hephaestus Mons and I wanted to learn the guiding landmarks.

CHAPTER 20

The mechanics completed their job on schedule, so the next evening I inspected their simple biplane. I would be satisfied if it managed to take me to Christianshus and no further. Daniel Szenes tested the engine and it responded with the desired roar. Linda had designed a radio-controlled fuse for the bomb and a booby-trap that would detonate it if someone tried to unfasten the lid.

I dressed myself for the bitter cold of the sky by putting on layer after layer of wool and cotton, with a windproof oilskin coat outmost. Flat hot-water bottles were added in appropriate places. Linda made a final check of the plane: everything in proper order.

I climbed into the cockpit, feeling clumsy like a baby. Linda handed me a cup of water and five pills in different colours, an unhealthy mix of medicaments that would make any doctor furious. If I survived this escapade, I would be knocked out for days with a serious risk of kidney injuries.

"The street is empty," Jacob called from beyond the yard's front fence.

Daniel and Victor opened the gate and pushed the plane into the street. The darkness was no problem, because my drug-enhanced sight registered everything of importance. Forty yards of asphalt ahead of me: sufficient, because the biplane's broad wings provided plenty of lift.

Linda came up next to me with the electro-starter. "Johnny, do come back," she called.

She looked unexpectedly feminine in a dirty overall, with smudged hands and a bad crew-cut. "See you," I said. I could not reach her for a handshake, so I merely winked and put the goggles over my eyes.

"Hals- und Beinbruch," she said and started the engine with a jolt.

116

I turned the throttle and the plane raced toward the end of the street. Ten yards, twenty yards, thirty yards – I pulled the stick. The plane took off and crossed the roof of a stone house with little clearance.

Fredriksborg quickly turned into a dark maze below me. The police would probably get reports soon about an alien aircraft, but I was already outside their reach. The Danish fighter planes could not find me in the darkness. I spotted the railway station and put the plane on the route to Christianshus.

The drugs harried my body and the cold cut to the bones. Several times I had to urinate in an improvised diaper. I soon lost the sense of time – cosmos shrunk to my cramped cockpit and the unceasing clamour of the engine. Keeping a steady course demanded all my energy. The weather remained calm, so I was spared hard winds or rain. The sky was mostly clear and the bright Canopus aided me whenever I wanted to double-check my course.

All suffering has an end. The moment arrived when I glimpsed the distant line where the mainland touched the ice sheet. I swallowed another pill to get more alert and pulled the stick to gain altitude. I did not want to be the target of trigger-happy soldiers. Sparks on the ground – scouts and sentries who fired rifles and machine guns at each other – showed me the extent of the battle area.

The Japanese encircled Christianshus completely. My engine alerted gunners on both sides and tracer bullets rose in arcs from the ground. However, they did not unsettle my artificial composure. The drugs in my blood dulled all emotions: the thought of killing thousands of people did not sicken me; it was just a job that I had decided to do.

I made a curve over the ice sheet and turned back toward Christianshus. When I flew over the terminal complex, I pulled a lever. The plane skipped upward at the release of the bomb. I leaned over the cockpit frame and watched its parachute unfold. I pushed the stick forward to put the plane into a shallow dive and increase its speed, because I needed to put a good distance between myself and the bomb before it exploded.

The railroad became my guide once again. After about ten miles I crossed a ridge and spotted a field that might serve as a landing strip. I cut the speed and turned. The wind came sidewise from an uncomfortable angle and made the plane waver. I put her down with such force that the fuselage trembled and creaked. It bumped forward and lost speed, but suddenly the wind seized the wings. The plane rolled over. I pressed the radio trigger – the mission must be concluded before I died.

A new sun shone behind me while the plane tumbled to the left. Long shadows and bright contrast filled my vision. The ground shattered the plane and mauled me. Pain and heat pushed a scream through my lips.

I crawled away from the wreckage, panting from anguish. A mottled fire ball flamed against the black sky – cremating or crushing thousands of people at Christianshus.

A shock wave hurtled across the field and tossed the wreck through the air. I pressed myself against the ground to avoid flying debris.

Mission accomplished: Christianshus obliterated, Fredriksborg saved. The war would continue, but nothing would remain the same: Humpty Dumpty sat on a wall, Humpty Dumpty had a great fall, all the king's horses and all the king's men couldn't put Humpty together again.

Soon the effects of the drugs wore off and the withdrawal made me vomit and weep. My left arm was so badly injured that I could not move it without crying from pain. Like the Greek god Phaeton, I had ruined a world with the sun's sky chariot and like him I had paid for it.

I crept inch by inch toward the railroad tracks, because that was the only place where rescuers could find me.

The real sun rose into the sky when I reached the tracks, but dawn brought no relief. The whole day I prayed that darkness would overwhelm me and take the pains away, but I did not lose consciousness for a moment. I lay on my back next to the railway ballast and followed the sun's arc across the sky. Monsters crawled around me in incomprehensible hallucinations. Coarse black grass prodded my back. Foulness leaked from my body, gradually turning me into stinking offal.

After a few hours a Danish fighter biplane flew past me high in the sky. It circled several times around the smoke pillars rising from Christianshus and then returned toward Fredriksborg. The pilot could not have seen me.

Afternoon came and the sun started to descend. My canteen kept thirst at bay. Far away I heard the clanking of an approaching train, but I could not turn my head in that direction. They'll see me, they'll see me, I prayed as the sound increased.

Brakes screeched and the engine stopped. Four Danish soldiers lifted me into a car and put me on an examination table. A nurse inspected my injuries.

"Give me no medicines," I whispered in Swedish. "I'm chock full with drugs." She put a splint around my left arm while I screamed with pain.

A convoy of four trains rolled slowly onwards to the place where Surtr had danced. I dozed off in a shaky bunk inside an improvised hospital car.

EPILOGUE

I spent three weeks recuperating in a locked wing of the State Hospital in Fredriksborg together with ill deserters and other criminals. The police explained that I had been arrested under the state-of-war regulations. I simulated amnesia and provided no explanation why I had been found next to the railway track. The doctors told me that my left arm had been permanently maimed, but that I otherwise should recover.

One day I was released by an order signed by the chief of police. The Danish authorities had decided that keeping a mentally disturbed but otherwise harmless man locked up was a waste of resources. It was after all not possible to charge me with any crime, because no one ever connected me to the transuranium explosion.

The wrecked aircraft and my backpack remained at the crash site and I think that nobody ever paid attention to them. What importance do you ascribe to fragments of metal and wood in a field when a huge crater smoulders nearby?

Daniel Szenes had contacted the police immediately after my departure from Fredriksborg and reported that an unidentified plane had landed and started in the adjacent street, The police obtained several contradictory witness reports, but failed to put together what really had transpired that evening so the case was soon dismissed.

The *Cassiopeia* left for Magalhana while I was hospitalized. Leclerc came to see me the day before her departure and asked what I wanted to report to colonel Ter Horst. I gave him a summary and told him to make sure that the colonel received Yazov's metal bars and the papers from the ancient mine.

Rumours circulating in the hospital claimed that the Japanese had taken some sort of doomsday weapon to Christianshus where it had detonated prematurely and wiped out both sides. The local newspapers published several unreliable and contradictory stories within a few days. People mentioned that ten thousand soldiers had perished, but I do not think that anybody will find out the correct number.

I never saw the devastated area with my own eyes, but that did not ease the burden on my conscience. I was personally responsible for the greatest mass murder in human history and ought to be hanged as a war criminal, because I had not been a legal combatant serving in a military force. But who would charge me? Only half a dozen people in Alba knew the truth and none of them would speak to the police. What conclusions did the governments in Tokyo, Saint Petersburg, Paris and Vienna draw? Only the future may tell. That also applies to the archaeological discoveries in the mine.

Regardless of those issues the Japanese expeditionary corps in Alba had been completely destroyed, as had most of the Russian and Danish forces. The ruthless Terboven used the situation to consolidate his gains, but he lacked resources for a lengthy aggressive war. Hence the great rebellion petered out in Alba, but raged on unabated elsewhere in the world – the samurai could not yet put his katana on the wall above the fireplace.

ABOUT THE AUTHOR

Anders Blixt is a political science and modern languages graduate from Lund University, Sweden. He has worked as a science journalist covering radiation protection and crisis management issues, served in civilian positions in multinational nation-building operations (e.g. in Afghanistan), and written two books about United Nations' military observer missions in Asia. Since the 1980s, he is also a professional designer of roleplaying games and he has created and developed dozens of titles for Swedish and US publishers. In 2011 he published his first novels in Swedish.

Currently Anders lives in Stockholm with wife and three children and works as a tech writer in the IT industry. He enjoys role-playing games with his friends and keeps a keen eye on the exploration of the solar system, in particular NASA's Mars rovers.

Anders blogs about books, games, and space research at *The Dream Forge* (http://gondica.wordpress.com).

www.ingramcontent.com/pod-product-compliance
Lightning Source LLC
Chambersburg PA
CBHW070753120626
46557CB00002B/573